A HOME FULL OF HOPE

BOOK FOUR OF THE NIGHTINGALE FAMILY SERIES

FENELLA J. MILLER

Boldwood

First published in 2018 as *All's Well That Ends Well*. This edition first published in Great Britain in 2024 by Boldwood Books Ltd.

Cover Design by Colin Thomas

Cover Photography: Colin Thomas and Alamy

A CIP catalogue record for this book is available from the British Library.

Paperback ISBN 978-1-83518-713-5

Large Print ISBN 978-1-83518-712-8

Hardback ISBN 978-1-83518-711-1

Ebook ISBN 978-1-83518-714-2

Kindle ISBN 978-1-83518-715-9

Audio CD ISBN 978-1-83518-706-7

MP3 CD ISBN 978-1-83518-707-4

Digital audio download ISBN 978-1-83518-708-1

Boldwood Books Ltd
23 Bowerdean Street
London SW6 3TN
www.boldwoodbooks.com

AUTHOR'S NOTE

The characters in this story are an accurate reflection of the time they are living in. As such, their thoughts, speech and actions are normal for this era. Thankfully we now live in a more enlightened time.

1

CHELMSFORD, AUGUST, AUGUST 1848

'Ma, Jimmy's eating dirt again,' Tommy yelled from the garden.

Alfie had been feeding the chickens and was supposedly keeping an eye on his youngest son. He loved both of them, but it weren't enough to keep him content. Betty was blooming and had made several suggestions about him moving back into the marital bed. He didn't want no more kids – two were enough for him.

'Shut it, Tommy, your ma's out at the market.' He rescued the infant and scooped the mud from his mouth. 'It ain't good for you, little man. Why don't you play with them bricks instead? Tommy, you're supposed to be playing with your brother.'

His oldest, now close to three years of age, scowled at him. 'I want to go with Joe, Davie and John. I don't like it here with you.'

'You ain't old enough to go out with your cousins – little Mary's satisfied with staying here, and she's older than you.'

The baby wriggled to be put down and he was happy to oblige. It were stupid arguing with a kiddie. In fact, his whole life were stupid. He had no place in this household although his ma, wife and sister did their best to make him feel important. Betty took care of the house – she had two skivvies to help her. His sister, Sarah, ran the clothes business and did the cutting and designing, whilst Ma oversaw the sewing and sale of the garments.

He flexed his damaged hand. If that bastard Hatch hadn't got his men to bust it, he would still be making decent furniture, have his own business, not be kept by the womenfolk. His only solace was his dog, Buster, and he wasn't looking too clever lately. He thought his huge friend felt as trapped as he did, living in the centre of Chelmsford and away from the countryside they both loved.

'Pa, Jimmy stinks.'

This was one job Alfie refused to do. Changing shit-filled rags was a woman's job. 'Right, you watch him; I'll fetch your Auntie Sarah.'

He didn't like to go inside the pristine back hallway without taking off his boots so he yelled through the open door.

'Sarah, Jimmy needs changing.'

She appeared from the office. 'You will have to bring him to the door. I'm not going out in my indoor shoes.'

Reluctantly he picked up the smelly baby and, holding him at arm's length, carried him to the back door. 'I'm taking the dogs for a walk; Tommy can come with me.'

Her smile faded. She was looking over his shoulder and he turned with a dreadful sinking feeling in his guts. Buster was stretched out by the back gate and Buster's son, Spot, was standing over him whining.

He ran to the animal's side and dropped to his knees. Buster opened an eye, licked his hand, thumped his tail once and with a sigh he was gone. Spot began to howl, an unearthly, hideous noise that brought the five seamstresses, skivvies, his ma and sister to the garden.

Alfie let the tears trickle unheeded down his cheeks. He'd just lost the most important friend in his life. Buster had been with him for seven years. He was the reason he was still living in Chelmsford. Sarah put her hand on his shoulder but he shrugged it off.

'I'm so sorry, Alfie, I know he meant the world to you, but he was old. It was his time to go – we all knew that.'

He scrambled to his feet. 'I need to bury him – but not here; we both hate it here. I'll take him to the river and bury him there.'

'You can't carry him. He's a deadweight; you'll never be able to pick him up. I'll send one of the girls for the carter, shall I?'

'I'll fetch him meself. I ain't completely useless. I'll cover him. I don't want the children upset.'

She leant past him and gently draped an old tablecloth over his friend. Spot had stopped howling and pressed himself against his leg. 'I know – it won't be the same now he's gone.'

He went through the house tramping mud down the freshly scrubbed flagstones and stormed out of the front door, slamming it behind him.

It were market day so he'd find a lad with a barrow easy enough. He hoped he didn't bump into his wife – she was the last person he wanted to share his grief with. Although the square was busy he soon found what he needed.

'You two, want to earn a bob for an hour's work?'

'Yeah, mister, too right,' the larger of the lads said eagerly.

'Bring your barrow. Follow me.' Alfie didn't explain why he needed them; he was too choked to talk about it even to strangers.

The garden was silent, no sign of his children. Spot was also absent, no longer guarding his dead father.

'We'll have to lift him on the cloth. It'll take all three of us.'

'Blimey, mister, he ain't half big. Where are we taking him?' Again, it was the larger of the two boys who spoke.

'Along the river. He liked it down there.'

Even with help it was bloody difficult getting the deadweight onto the barrow but eventually they managed it. He left them to push and strode ahead with a shovel on his shoulder. He stopped where the river curved, where it were quiet and Buster could rest in peace.

'Just put him there, then you two can bugger off.' He tossed them a coin each and they seemed satisfied with the exchange. He waited until he was alone before beginning to dig the hole in the bank. It had to be high up as the river flooded and he didn't want his dog's remains washed into the water.

First, he carefully cut away the grass and rolled it up so he could replace it after Buster was buried. It were going to take a bleeding big hole. He'd been digging for an hour when footsteps approached. He didn't look round. Hoped whoever it was would have the common courtesy to walk past without comment.

A hand dropped on his shoulder. 'Right sorry about Buster, Uncle Alfie. We're here to help,' Joe, his oldest nephew, said from behind him.

'Thanks, lads, appreciate it.'

With all four of them digging, the grave was completed in another hour and they reverently rolled Buster's remains into the hole. Then they backfilled and replaced the top grass.

'I don't reckon anyone would know he was there, Uncle Alfie,' Davie said.

'Spot wouldn't come with us. He's hiding in the pantry,' John added.

Alfie brushed the worst of the mud from his trousers, cleaned the shovel on the grass, and was ready to go. He'd not come down here again, not ever. He'd said his goodbyes.

'You'd better get back. Your ma will have tea on the table.'

'Aren't you coming, Uncle?'

'No, Joe, I need to be on me own. Tell your Auntie Betty not to wait up for me.'

The three boys huddled together, staring at him as if he were a stranger. He put his arms around them. It weren't their fault Buster had kicked the bucket. They had loved him as much as he had and must be as devastated as he was.

'He meant a lot to me, boys. He saved my life a dozen times. I don't know how I'm going to manage without him.'

John, the youngest at eight years of age, sniffed and wiped his snotty nose on his sleeve. 'We've still got Spot. You ain't got no one now.'

'Don't be daft, our John, Uncle Alfie's got all of us. And he can share Spot, can't he?'

'Joe's right – I'm not thinking straight. You run along. I'll see you later. I thank you for your help.'

Alfie's voice was gruff. He turned his back on them and strode away, not wanting them to see him cry.

* * *

Sarah heard the door slam and swallowed the lump in her throat. Her brother would take this loss badly, indeed they all would. No, that wasn't quite true, as Betty had never taken to Buster. Tommy was crying and Jimmy struggling to get down.

'No, I need to change your backside. Tommy, go and find Mary. She's helping your grandma in the shop.'

The little boy ran off, his tears forgotten as he wasn't allowed out there. He usually knocked things over if not watched every second.

The maids were still snivelling. 'Get about your work, you two – no excuse for standing about.'

They scuttled off leaving her with the unpleasant task of a very smelly baby to deal with. Her mother brought both children into the back parlour, the one they used for every day. 'I've just heard about the dog. Alfie's already unsettled. Losing his best friend might be the last straw.'

'He and Betty don't get along too well. He's fond of his boys, but I don't think that's enough to keep him here. I think he might well leave now Buster has gone.'

'He doesn't like the fact that we bring in the money with our business. You'd think that he'd be happy to swagger about in smart clothes with nothing to do all day. Most men would be.'

'Alfie's not like most men. He's always looked after himself and his family. It sits hard with him that he can't make his cabinets any more. He's never loved Betty, not really; he wouldn't have married her if she hadn't been in the family way.'

'He offered to invest his own money in my business but I told him to keep it.'

Sarah stared at her mother. 'I didn't know that. Small wonder he's not happy with the situation. Why wouldn't you let him put money in?'

Her mother pulled a face. 'He didn't make that money honestly. I don't want it anywhere near my business.'

This was the second time Ma had called it her business – Sarah had thought it was a joint enterprise. After all, without her design skills and financial acumen the shop wouldn't have become as lucrative as it was.

'Too late to repine. The damage has been done. If Alfie leaves it will be your fault.'

'It wouldn't make any difference if he did go. He's just another mouth to feed, and he doesn't bring in any money of his own. Why doesn't he make the things that he can? Those baby chairs, beds and such would sell.'

This conversation was going badly. It was as if she didn't know her mother, yet she had been working closely with her for the past two years, building up the ladies' and children's ready-made clothing business. Ma owned the lease for the premises, but before Sarah had joined her she had only been making a fraction of what they were now.

'He hasn't got a workshop, he had to leave his tools behind, and when he asked if he could build something in the garden you refused to let him.'

'There's barely enough room out there for the children to play, to hang out the laundry and such – I didn't want a blooming great shed taking up half the space.'

'In which case why are you complaining he hasn't been doing any carpentry? He tried to find himself premises close by but the only place that was suitable was the other side of Chelmsford and Betty kicked up a fuss when he suggested they moved there. I went to see the house myself and it was perfect.'

'That girl knows which side her bread is buttered, Sarah – she wouldn't have servants to do her bidding anywhere else.'

The front door opened and closed; Betty came in and her happy smile slipped. The maid, carrying two laden baskets, staggered past and on into the kitchen. 'Why the gloomy faces?'

'Buster died. Alfie's taking it hard.'

'He thought more of that animal than he does of his wife and children. Maybe now he'll consider being a proper husband to me.'

'Betty, how can you be so callous? Buster was with him for years; he had a bond with that dog that was quite remarkable. If you don't want to lose him altogether you'd better change your attitude. He needs our support and sympathy.' Her comment struck home.

'You can't mean that, Sarah – surely he wouldn't abandon his family because his dog has died?'

She glanced at her mother. 'Ma refused to let him be part of this business; you refused to move when he found somewhere suitable to work. He doesn't have a place here. He needs to earn his own living and not be dependent on us. I don't know why you don't understand this.'

Her mother finally took notice. 'If I'd known how badly he took it I would never have refused him. You tell him he can put his money into this business and I'll put his name on the deeds.'

'It might be too late for that; he's had the past two years to stew about things. He told me last month that he was thinking of going to London to look for his old friend and maybe go into business with him.'

Betty burst into noisy tears. 'Don't let him go, Sarah. Tell him I'll move wherever he wants as long as he stays.'

'Why are you asking *me* to do this? Betty, he's your husband. Ma, he's your son. I can't put matters right for you. This is something you have to do yourselves.'

'I've got to get back to the shop, Sarah. I heard the bell go three times. I'll speak to him when he gets back from burying that dog.'

Her mother rushed off leaving her with her sister-in-law, who was still sniffing loudly. 'The boys will be back from school soon. They're going to be desperately sad.'

'Won't you speak to Alfie for me? Tell him what a good wife I am, that I love him, that he has a duty to stay with us?'

'No, that's something you must do yourself. I'll leave you to take care of the children. I've got business to attend to.'

Once in the sanctuary of her office she had time to think about the consequences of what had happened this morning. She should have spoken to Betty and her mother months ago, then maybe things would not be as parlous as they were. She feared whatever anyone said to her brother it was too late and he would depart.

Last time he had gone to London he had been sold as a slave to a lighterman, had eventually escaped with Buster, and lived a life of crime on the streets until he had made enough to set himself up in a small business delivering items on barrows.

When he'd returned to Colchester he had been a man of means, although not yet sixteen years of age. If Dan, her beloved husband, hadn't been killed in a tragic accident none of this would have happened. Although two years had passed since her man had died she still missed him dreadfully – especially as every time his son Joe stepped into the room she was reminded of him.

Her eldest stepson was now, at twelve, almost a man, his shoulders beginning to widen, his voice to deepen, and he was now as tall as she was. Davie, a year younger, took after his dead ma, was slight of build and fairer of colouring. John, now eight, was like neither of them. His hair was a sandy colour and his eyes were green. However, there was no mistaking that they were siblings.

The daughter she'd had with Dan looked like her, apart from the fact that her hair was more black than brown. Now she was almost three years old, as bright as a button, and a constant delight. Living in a house full of boys she was petted and fussed but miraculously had remained unspoiled by all this attention.

Whatever Betty and her ma thought, she believed Alfie should go to London. It would be better if he departed with everyone's blessing as that way he was more likely to stay in touch. If he left in high dudgeon he might not come back and that she couldn't bear.

She kept watch for her boys and was on her feet to greet them as soon as they opened the back gate. They were joshing and laughing as they crossed the garden. She hated to be the one to spoil their good mood.

'Boys, Buster died this morning. Your uncle is burying him somewhere along the riverbank.'

'We were talking about that yesterday. We knew he didn't have long. I reckon Uncle Alfie will be knocked sideways. Come along, you two, grab some spades. We'll go and find him. Give him a hand.'

'Where's Spot? We'll take him with us.'

'I don't know, Davie; he's hiding somewhere. I should try the scullery.'

He hurried off whilst his brothers were collecting the tools they needed to help dig the hole. He returned shaking his head. 'He won't come. We'll have to go without him.'

'Boys, don't be surprised if your uncle is a bit brusque with you. He'll appreciate you being there even if he doesn't say so.'

They exchanged glances and nodded. 'We ain't stupid, Ma; we know how much Buster meant to him. We loved him too, but it ain't the same for us.' Joe smiled sadly and led the two younger boys out of the gate without a further word.

She was proud of her boys. They were getting a good education and when Joe left school this summer he was hoping to sign up as a cabin boy. Robert Billings, a good friend of her brother's and of hers, was a first mate and had already passed his captain's ticket. He'd promised to find Joe a place on his vessel.

She would have to be blind not to know that Robert was in love with her. He never said or did anything to cause her offence when he visited, but just knowing when she was ready he was there gave her hope for the future.

2

Alfie wanted to drown his sorrows but couldn't face going into an alehouse when he was so distressed. He needed to go somewhere quiet where he could think. He'd buy himself a pasty and a coffee, then come back here. There was always a coffee stall in the market and more than one place he could find himself a decent pie.

He had lived in Chelmsford for almost two years but hadn't made any friends. His mate, Robert, caught the train from Colchester whenever he had shore leave, but he'd not been around for the last year and he'd missed him. He thought his friend was sweet on his sister, and they'd make a good match, but he didn't reckon Sarah was ready to move on from Dan just yet.

Once he'd got his grub he headed for the river again, but the opposite bank to the one upon which he'd just buried his best friend. There was nothing to keep him here now. Betty was well provided for and so were his sons. Sarah didn't need him; her business was thriving and she was putting large sums of money every week into a bank account.

When he'd been living in London a few years back he'd made a good friend, apart from Jimmy who died, one George Benson. It were he who'd taught him carpentry. He hadn't seen him for years, had not been back to the city, but he would go now and search out George and see if he couldn't invest in his business. He wouldn't return until he had made something of himself, could hold his head up, provide for his wife and family himself.

He'd speak to Sarah first – she was the only one who understood him. He still had his money in the bank. He'd get it transferred to a London branch – he wasn't stupid enough to carry it in his pocket like what he had all those years ago.

Decision made, he returned to the house that had never been his home, the place where he'd always felt like an intruder, an unwanted lodger. He didn't object to women earning their own keep, running a business, but it were a man's job to provide and nobody could tell him otherwise.

He hesitated at the back gate, knowing the pain would strike him like a knife when he opened it. His beloved Buster had died there and he would have to walk past the place he'd drawn his last breath. Too late to walk around to the front, he might as well go in. There were too many bad memories here now – the sooner he left the happier he'd be.

His sister was waiting for him in the passageway and beckoned him into her office where they wouldn't be disturbed. The children knew better than to go in there unless invited. He could hear the murmur of voices coming from the parlour. Nobody but him seemed to have been adversely affected by this loss.

'You've decided to go haven't you, Alfie?'

His sister had always understood him best. 'I have. I'm not going to sneak off like a thief in the night. I'll speak to Betty and Ma, but I'm off tomorrow. I've got to visit the bank, but after that I'm catching the next train to London.'

'Promise me you'll keep in touch. I know why you've got to do this. I don't think you're right, but I do understand. As long as you let us know where you are then I expect we can manage without you for a while.'

'I'm not coming back until I've made something of meself. I'm sick of being looked down on, laughed at. I need to be able to hold my head up...'

'There's no need to exaggerate, Alfie. Nobody looks down on you or laughs at you. It's in your own imagination. At least be honest with yourself about the reasons you're going.'

His cheeks flushed and he ran a finger around his collar. 'I ain't happy with Betty. I should never have married her, let alone had two kids. I'm no good as a father or husband. They'll be better off without me. I only stayed for you and Buster.'

'Not for our mother?'

'She ain't what you think she is, Sarah – you want to watch her. Put some money in your own name so that it ain't all in hers. You're doing the hard work; make sure you have something put by just in case.'

'I think you could be right, but I hope not. The children love her and she has treated Dan's boys as if they were her own grandchildren. That said, in future I will put half the money in my name.'

'Do that, Sarah love. You don't want to end up with nothing after all the hard work you've put in over the past two years. I've always thought she could have made more of an effort to find us if she'd really wanted to.'

'That's water under the bridge, but I never want to be in the same situation I was when Dan died. I've got four dependents to consider now. What do you think will happen to Betty and your sons if our mother abandons us again?'

'I don't expect you to provide for my family. I won't be living here, but I'll send funds for them as soon as I'm set up. It ain't that far; I can be back in a couple of hours.'

'That's all right then. Explain to Betty that you intend to come back. She'll not be happy, but she'll accept it as long as she knows you'll be home one day. Come for your boys' birthdays, for Christmas perhaps – as you say, it's only an hour or so on the train.'

'I can do that. I ain't exactly running away, just going off to make something of myself. I ain't comfortable being supported by you and Ma.'

As always talking things through with his sister made it clearer in his head. She didn't judge him, nag him, make him feel inferior like what Betty and his ma did. Until she'd mentioned it he hadn't thought about coming back to see everyone until he was financially secure again.

'I'm transferring half my money to London but I'll put the rest in your account to take care of Betty and the boys if need be. Don't tell her – she'll fritter it away, knowing her. I take it you have one?'

'I certainly do – I've been putting a pound or two away each week for a rainy day.' She wrote the numbers on a slip of paper and handed it to him.

'As soon as you have settled, send us your address. In fact, make sure you write once a week even if it's only a few words.'

'I'll do that. I ain't one for writing as you know, but for you I'll make the effort.' He stood up and she did too. He embraced her knowing that whatever he'd just said to the contrary it were likely to be a long time before he saw her again. He wanted a clean break, to start again and make something of himself.

He didn't fancy socialising so went upstairs and packed the items he intended to take with him. He heard Betty putting his boys to bed but didn't go in to them. He waited until she came out of the children's room and then called her name.

She pushed open the door and saw his bag. 'I knew it. You're leaving us aren't you?'

He was about to explain his reasons, that he would come and visit, that he would write but she gave him no chance to speak.

'You've never loved me. That blooming dog's come first and Sarah second – me and the boys are last in your affections. You go – you're no use or ornament to me. I'll be glad to see the back of you, Alfie Nightingale.' She turned and stamped out, her nose in the air. Even then, in her fury, she remembered not to slam the door and wake the children.

He heard Sarah come up, which meant that his ma would be downstairs on her own. He wanted to get a few things straight with her before he left in the morning.

* * *

When Sarah went down the next morning her brother had already gone. The house seemed empty somehow without Buster or Alfie.

'Come along, Spot, you can't hide under there any longer. You need to go out in the garden and do your business.'

The dog sidled out on his belly, ignored his full food bowl, but slipped out of the door when she held it open. The two kitchen maids were already busy at their duties, so she had a precious half an hour to herself before her daughter woke.

She spent the time checking the stock in the sewing room, making note of what was needed for the orders in hand. By the time this was done the seamstresses had arrived, chattering and laughing as if today was like any other day. For them, of course, the loss of the dog and Alfie would make no difference at all.

Breakfast was quieter than usual but apart from that it was as if nothing untoward had taken place yesterday. Even her boys were acting as if they didn't care. It would appear that only the remaining dog and herself were affected.

Betty was talking brightly about a forthcoming play that was to be performed locally. Her mother didn't eat breakfast and was already overseeing the girls in the workroom. Then her daughter banged on the table with her spoon.

'Where's my Uncle Alfie and big dog Buster? I don't like it here without them.'

The words hung in the air; the atmosphere changed. Tommy began to cry, Jimmy joined in and then Betty began to sob too. Her boys dropped their cutlery, pushed back their chairs with such violence two of them crashed to the flagstones, and they ran out of the back door without their midday snack.

Sarah wanted to join in the general wailing and crying but swallowed the lump in her throat. 'Betty, you're upsetting the children. Mary love, your uncle has gone away for a bit on business and your big friend Buster has gone to join your pa in heaven.'

Betty dried her eyes on her sleeve and used the edge of the tablecloth to mop the faces of her boys. 'That's right, your pa will be back to see you soon enough. Buster was old and sick. He's running around like a puppy now with your Uncle Dan.'

Hearing these platitudes from both herself and Betty was enough to stop the racket. Tommy picked up a spoon and continued to eat his porridge. Mary was not so easily placated. She looked around the table and then fixed her eyes on her.

'I don't like Buster being with our pa. I want him to come back. I don't want Uncle Alfie to be with Pa.'

'No, sweetheart, he's not in heaven. He's gone to London on business.

Now, finish your breakfast and I'll take you and Tommy for a walk along the river. What about that?'

This was enough to distract her daughter. Betty ate nothing; neither did she. It would be some time before her appetite returned.

'Where is Spot, Sarah? I can't see him in the garden.'

Sure enough, the garden was empty apart from the chickens in their run at the far end. 'He must have gone with the boys. They'll bring him home when they come at lunchtime. I'm sure he'll wait quietly in the yard outside the school until they come out again.'

'I hope you're right, but he's never done that before and I think one of them would have brought him back.'

'There's nothing we can do about it now. I've got a meeting this afternoon at a warehouse, so I'd better get off if I'm going to be back in time.'

With Betty's help the little ones were soon ready for their walk. When she suggested they go to the river and feed the ducks with stale bread they were overjoyed at the idea. Once they were safely through the town and away from the diligences, carriages and barrows, she let the children walk without holding her hands.

'Ma, can we run?' Mary asked as she hopped from one foot to the other.

'Not by the river, sweetheart, just in case you fall in.'

Her younger brother Tommy had fallen into the River Colne in Colchester and drowned. He'd been a bit older than these two, but it had destroyed the family. Her stepfather had blamed her for not keeping an eye on him and Alfie had run away. This was seven years ago, but being by the river with small children brought it painfully to mind.

Even letting Tommy and Mary walk sedately in front of her was almost too much. She didn't want to go too far as she knew how long it would take to feed the ducks and didn't want to be late for her important meeting. Whilst she was out she intended to call in at the bank and see if Alfie had kept his word.

'I can see a lot of ducks on the other side of the river, children, so this will be a good place to throw the bread to them.' They were now about a mile from the town. The path was quiet with only the sound of the birds and the gentle lapping of the river against the bank to break the peace.

The children had a small cloth bag each full of crusts. She had brought a piece of old towelling for them to sit on whilst they threw the bread. They would be much safer on their bottoms than dancing around on the edge.

Then Mary squealed in excitement. 'Look, Ma, I can see Spot up there on the bank. Why is he lying there?'

Sarah knew at once. This must be where Buster was buried, but she could hardly tell them this.

'Why don't you call him? You know how he loves bread. I think he might come to us if he knows we've got plenty to give him.'

Mary tugged at her skirt. 'He's sad, Ma, 'cos Buster's gone.'

'I think he is, sweetheart, but we'll just have to be extra nice to him until he gets over it.'

She positioned herself between the water and the children whilst they jumped up and down and shouted for the dog to come. It was amazing to see the animal respond so rapidly. From dejected to delighted in the space of seconds.

'He's coming, he's coming. I want to give him everything. Them old ducks can wait till next time,' Tommy yelled.

The dog bounded up to them and covered the children in wet, slobbery kisses. He didn't seem too bothered about the bread, was just pleased to see them.

They spent a happy hour throwing bread into the river, which was left to sink in a soggy mass as the ducks had more sense than to come over with the dog there. They threw sticks into the water and Spot jumped in to retrieve them.

'I'm going to dry your hands first, children, and then give the dog a rub-down.'

'Spot's happy again, Auntie Sarah, ain't he?'

'He is, Tommy; he had a grand time today.'

On the way back the animal walked at her side, pressing close. She hadn't the heart to push him away, even though her gown was soaking by the time they reached the garden gate. What the children hadn't understood was that the dog had somehow scaled the fence – it would no longer be safe to leave him unattended in the garden, which was a nuisance. She really didn't want to have to tie him up.

Her mother was tight-lipped about Alfie's departure and Betty pretended everything was fine and her husband would be home in a day or two. It was true that they could manage perfectly well to run the business without him being there, but a home without a man at its head was somehow incomplete.

That afternoon she put on her best bonnet, her smartest gown, and set out to visit the only bank in the town. The small counter, behind which stood two tellers, occupied the far end of the room. It was hardly a grand affair, little more than a branch office. She came in so frequently she was recognised and greeted by name.

'I bid you good morning, Mrs Cooper. How can I be of assistance today?'

'I need to speak to Mr Crickett if he is available?' He was one of the directors of this bank and was usually around in the morning.

She was ushered with due ceremony into the small office at the rear of the building. Once she was seated she explained the reason for her visit.

'I can confirm, Mrs Cooper, that Mr Nightingale deposited twenty-five guineas in your account yesterday. Do you wish to know the balance?'

'I do indeed. That is the main reason I have come in. I have also a deposit for the account of Mrs Rand and another one for my own account.'

She was pleased to hear she would have just over fifty pounds with the two she was adding today. 'Thank you, Mr Crickett. I shall be depositing in both accounts in future.'

He knew better than to comment on the change of arrangement. She stood, he did also, and she bid him good day. As long as Ma didn't go into the bank herself and ask to see her balance she could see no difficulty putting money aside for herself and her family.

The silk merchants showed her their latest samples and she made her order. They were now getting not only the less well-off coming in to buy ready-made clothes, but also the more well-to-do. Word had spread that the latest fashions could be purchased from their business at a fraction of the cost of having something made especially, to measure.

She shuddered as she remembered the appalling garments she had been obliged to wear before her beloved Dan had taken her under his wing. She could no longer recall his voice in her head, but seeing Joe every day kept his face fresh in her memory.

She stopped to pass the time of day with two acquaintances and was almost at her front door when there were heavy footsteps behind her. Her heart lifted. Alfie had changed his mind and come back to them. She spun and saw not her brother, but Robert Billings, a gentleman almost as dear to her. Robert was more than two yards high, handsome in a rugged sort of way, but his most unusual feature was his startlingly red hair.

'Sarah, I'm glad I caught you. Must you go in immediately or can we take a stroll along the river? I need to talk to you in private.'

'How is it that you always know when you are most needed? I have much to tell you as well.'

She put her arm through his and they walked in companionable silence along the edge of the River Can. 'We won't be able to walk along here as we do now when the new houses are finished. I hear the sewage is to go directly into the river. It will be most unpleasant as the river is scarcely wide enough to deal with it.'

He chuckled. 'You'll need to keep the dogs out of the water.'

She swallowed a lump in her throat at his mention of the dogs. 'Buster died yesterday and Alfie has gone to live in London. That's not all… I fear my mother does not consider me a true partner in the business as I have only invested my time and expertise, and not hard cash.'

She had his full attention now. 'I'm sorry to hear about Buster – he was a grand dog, I'm not surprised Alfie has taken off. He's not been happy here, having nothing valuable to do.'

'I told him he had my support as long as he keeps in touch. I pray he doesn't disappoint me in that respect.'

'Did you tell him your fears about the business and Mrs Rand?'

'He suggested I put money in my own account each week and not have it all go in my mother's.'

'A wise decision. However, Sarah, you'll never be without support as long as I'm alive. You know how I feel about you. I've waited two years to speak, but I'm hoping you'll consider taking me as your husband on my next leave.'

Sarah had known this question was coming but until he spoke had not known what her answer would be. 'I should love to marry you, Robert, but there are conditions to my acceptance. You must take all of us, or none. I wish to continue to work. I doubt I would be content as a lady of leisure.'

His roar of triumph sent hopeful ducks quacking into the air in disapproval. He grabbed her elbows and swung her around as if she weighed no more than a bag of feathers.

'Robert, put me down. I'm not a child.'

Instead of doing so he pulled her hard against his broad chest, his intentions clear. She wasn't sure she was ready to be kissed by him but he left her no option. He tilted her face up and covered her mouth with his.

She had expected feel the pleasant warmth she had always experienced when Dan had done the same. To her astonishment heat travelled from her toes to her crown and centred in her most private place. She leant against him, willingly opened her mouth and sailed into uncharted territories.

Finally, she understood what Betty had said years ago when they had discussed the intimacies of marriage. Her friend had insisted if there weren't tingles up and down her arms she wasn't doing it correctly. Kissing Robert was sending shock waves throughout her body. The sooner she could share his bed the better.

3

LONDON, 1848

Alfie had no regrets about departing. As far as he was concerned they would all be better off without him. He was just an extra mouth to feed and not bringing in any money. He was satisfied he'd done enough to ensure Betty and the boys were never destitute. Hopefully that wouldn't happen – but he didn't trust his ma as far as he could throw her.

He treated himself to an inside seat on the train. He were a smart gent now, well-pressed striped trousers, black topcoat, grey silk waistcoat and top hat. He also carried a cane with a silver top – this was for protection as much as anything else. He would be more comfortable in clothing less restrictive but looking like a toff was a disguise. He needed to be certain no one from his old life would recognise him.

On leaving the train he handed his ticket to the guard with a disdainful look just like the other coves what he had travelled with in first class. As long as he kept his trap shut he reckoned he could pass for a grand gent.

He emerged from the station and was staggered at the changes that had taken place in the few years since he had been here. The air was heavy with soot, the streets piled high with horse dung, which added to the stink. He left the Great Eastern Station and wandered into Brick Lane where Sclater Street traversed it. This was the market of the fancy – streets were blocked with folk coming to buy pigeons, canaries, rabbits, fowl, parrots and guinea pigs, indeed, anything to do with the keeping of birds or pets. Although the street was bustling it really came alive at night when by the flicker of gaslight those who had finished a day's work came out to buy their provender.

He brushed away unwanted moisture from his cheeks – he needed no reminder of what he had lost. He was pestered by sellers of shellfish pushing their barrows but he ignored them. He found the place where the cabriolets waited, one-horse carriages, which was for hire by moneyed gents like him.

'Where to, sir?' The jarvey touched his cap with his whip.

Alfie climbed in and doing so sharply reminded him of the only time he'd travelled in a hired carriage before. This had been when he was taken to say his goodbyes to his best mate Jimmy on his deathbed. His last connection to Jimmy had been Buster, and now he was gone too.

He gave the name of the street where George Benson had set up his workshop and settled back. He scarcely saw the houses, shops and pedestrians; he was lost in his own thoughts. George had intended to marry his sweetheart. They had set up the cottage that came with the workshop together. It were several years since he'd seen him, and he weren't even sure the cove still lived in the same place. If his business had been successful he might well have moved somewhere better.

The carriage lurched to a stop. He paid his dues and went in search of his friend. He didn't know the exact address but was sure he would recognise it when he found it. After wandering up and down for a while he saw the building he was looking for.

There were a smart sign over the archway that led into the yard but it didn't say Benson, but Radcliffe. This was definitely the place. He might as well enquire within. Whoever now owned it might have knowledge of his mate's whereabouts.

The sound of hammering and sawing filled the yard. There were a couple of apprentices sanding and polishing the finished articles and two carpenters working undercover. Neither of them stopped at his approach. He banged on the door until he got their attention.

'Excuse me, gents, I'm looking for George Benson, the bloke what used to own this place a few years back.'

The two, obviously brothers, exchanged glances. The older, with a hooked nose and bald pate, put down his chisel and came out to speak to him.

'It were a right shame. We bought this business from him three years ago. His missus and babe was taken with the sweating sickness and he took to the bottle. We'd been looking for a decent premises and stepped in. We gave him a fair price. I ain't sure where he went from here – but I don't reckon it were anywhere good.'

'Thank you for telling me. I wish I'd known. I could have helped him.'

They returned to their work and he left them to it. There was little point in searching for George. Once a bloke was on the downward slide he could be anywhere, living in the slums alongside others what were doing their best to drink themselves to death.

He would find himself lodgings in this neighbourhood but not dressed as he was – the landlady would charge him double. He had sufficient funds to keep him for a year or two if he were careful. The first thing to do was get out of these togs and into something he were more comfortable with. He'd sell his smart clothes; they'd fetch him a pretty penny.

He found a convenient alley and changed his raiment. Once wearing boots, flannel shirt, necktie and loose jacket he was less conspicuous and more comfortable. Now all he had to do was flog the other stuff and he could find himself a drum. He weren't interested in doing for himself; he needed lodgings what gave him full board, plus laundry and ironing done too.

After a short search he saw a vacancy sign in a three-storey house with a scrubbed front step, clean glass and crisply ironed curtains hanging at the windows. He strode up to the front door and hammered with the dolphin-shaped knocker.

The door was opened almost immediately by a girl in a mob cap and spotlessly clean apron. This was encouraging. She dipped in a curtsy.

'Can I help you, sir? Have you come about the room?'

'I have. Is your mistress in?'

'If you would follow me, mister, I'll take you to the parlour. She's out the back.'

The room he was shown to were overcrowded with highly polished oak furniture, every surface covered with knick-knacks and china ornaments. There were two stuffed birds under glass domes that took his eye. He was examining them when the woman he hoped would be his landlady sailed in.

'Good afternoon. Ellie tells me you are interested in my vacancy? I do not take riff-raff from the streets. I require evidence of good character before I allow any gentlemen into my establishment.'

Alfie understood what sort of woman she was. He pulled out his wallet and showed the rhino in it. 'I take it you wish me to pay a month in advance?'

Seeing he was a well-off gent was enough to change her attitude. 'Yes indeed. I am Mrs Digby, and you, sir?'

'Mr Alfie Nightingale, seeking a business to invest in.' He nodded and her thin lips turned up at the corners – not quite a smile but an improvement on her previous sour expression.

'My terms are two shillings a day all found...'

'I need to see the accommodation before I decide, Mrs Digby.'

He was shown a decent-sized room, well-furnished, with a view over the small backyard. It were ideal: clean and quiet. There were a bookcase – empty – a table and chair to do for his desk, and there was even enough room for a padded chair in front of the fireplace.

'Where's your facilities?'

'You will see you have a washstand. There's the necessary item in the commode for night use. The privy is in the yard. For an extra sixpence a week you can take a bath in the laundry room. Hot water will be provided in the morning, and a jug of cold left for the evening.'

'Right, I'll take it. Here's three guineas for the next month.' He dipped into his jacket and removed a cloth bag in which he kept his coins. He selected the necessary gold coins and dropped them into her outstretched hand. In fact, he was underpaying by a few bob but she was so impressed with his gesture she made no protest.

'Your evening meal can be served in your room or you can eat in the dining room with my other lodgers. It is at seven in order to allow those who are gainfully employed to return here. Breakfast is between six o'clock and seven thirty. I do not provide a midday repast as I do not expect my gentlemen to be here during the day.'

In other words, he'd have to go out if he wanted to eat. 'I'll eat in the dining room.'

She nodded and almost smiled before moving smoothly to the door and hurrying off about her daily business. He hadn't asked how many residents there were – no doubt he would discover this tonight. He doubted any of the fellers had manual work. They'd be clerks, office workers or something similar.

It didn't take long to unpack his carpetbag. Glad now he hadn't got around to selling his smart clothes, he rather thought he'd need them if he was going to find himself gainful employment. He could read well enough, but his writing was laboured. He wouldn't be taken on as a clerk.

He was a big man, strong and agile and could handle himself. He could probably find himself a position as a debt collector, but he weren't prepared to do something like that. There would certainly be similar employment to what he'd done for that bastard Hatch but he didn't want no illegal job, not this time.

Although he'd handed over the money as if he'd got rhino to burn – his twenty-five quid wouldn't last long if he remained here. He was out of touch with life in the city and feared he'd made a catastrophic error abandoning his family and coming here. But he weren't going crawling back with his tail between his legs. He'd not return until he'd made something of himself, so he'd better come up with something quick smart.

* * *

Chelmsford, 1848

Sarah pushed against Robert's chest until he released her. 'It doesn't seem right being so happy when Alfie has gone and Betty and the boys are on their own.'

'You've been on your own since Dan died. It's your turn to be looked after. I came to tell you that my next berth is a long one. I'll not be back for a year. It's India, then trading in the area before we return.'

'I'm content to wait. I'd like to move back to Colchester, unless you want to live here.'

'I'll be a captain when I get back. I'll purchase you, little Mary and the boys, a fine house in Lexden. You'll want for nothing. Which brings me to another reason I've come. There's a cabin boy's berth for Joe available now, but it will mean he'll have to leave with me this evening.'

The thought of losing her oldest son so suddenly was almost too much to deal with. 'The family is in disarray; with the loss of Buster and then Alfie moving to London, I'm not sure having Joe depart as well is a good idea.'

'It's not the best timing, but he's twelve years of age, and ready to start making his way in the world. The fact that he will be away for so long is another drawback for you all, but I'll be there to keep an eye on him. He'll not be allowed to be miserable.'

'I'll not stop him if he wants to go with you. As for being miserable, I doubt he'll have time to mope about. I just hope he doesn't suffer from seasickness.'

Robert's smile tilted her world. 'He'll be lucky if he doesn't, but he'll find his sea legs soon enough. What time are the boys back from school?'

'At one o'clock, so we have an hour or so to ourselves before they get home. Things are changing so fast for this family and there are matters we need to discuss before you leave.'

'The matter of our nuptials? Do you want to get married in Chelmsford or Colchester? Are you content to live in Lexden or do you have some other part of the town you would prefer? I've tried to persuade my ma to move somewhere more salubrious than St Botolph's but she's adamant she will remain in the house she was born in. I've spent a deal of money renovating and repairing it and it's a decent enough place.'

'As long as your younger brother and sisters get a good education it doesn't really matter where they are. I'm sure you will give them whatever they need when they are old enough to leave home.'

She smiled up at him. 'I don't need a grand house in the smartest part of the town, just somewhere with a garden where I can grow flowers and keep a few chickens.'

His arm tightened around her waist. 'I love you, Sarah Cooper, and I can't believe I'm finally going to get my dearest wish.' Then he frowned. 'What about your business here? Are you sure you want to leave it when it's so successful?'

'My mother has made it very clear she considers it all hers. Nothing is in my name. I should like to have my own concern, design and make clothes not only for the less well-off, but also for the grander folk. Until then I am gaining experience and don't resent being taken advantage of. Ma took us in when we were destitute and for that I'll be forever grateful.'

'Then I'll leave you to plan our wedding here. My family can travel up on the train and we can all stay at the Saracens – in fact, why don't you arrange for the wedding breakfast to be held there?'

'I'll do that, but there's no urgency as you won't be back until next year. As long as you let me know a few weeks before you dock that will be plenty of time to make the arrangements. Once we're married we can find ourselves a suitable home. I'm willing to move back to Colchester.'

Betty and her nephews might not be pleased to hear her news, especially in the present circumstances. As soon as she knew where her brother was lodging, she would send him the information and tell him he must return before she moved away. This would give him a year, quite long enough to realise where his duty lay.

After consideration they decided not to announce their engagement – Betty didn't need to have her nose rubbed in it. Plenty of time to do that next year, nearer the time. Sarah was happy to keep this secret to herself until then.

Robert had taken Joe into the garden to give him the news. This would allow the boy to refuse without embarrassment if he so wished.

Davie was watching out of the kitchen window. 'Joe looks right pleased with himself, Ma. I reckon Uncle Robert has found him a position on his ship.'

'You're very observant, young man. That's exactly why Robert came today. From what you say it would seem your brother intends to go with him. It will be hard saying goodbye, especially as this trip is to India and he won't be back for a year.'

'Uncle Robert will take care of him. I ain't worried about that.'

'Good, I was concerned you two would be very upset for him to go after what's happened.'

'Uncle Alfie will be back soon enough. Buster has been ailing for weeks so we were ready for his dying. John and me will miss Joe, but he's done nothing but talk about becoming a sailor for the past three years.'

Betty came in carrying Jimmy and with Mary and Tommy close behind her. 'What's that? Is your Joe leaving too? I never thought, when it came to it, he'd want to go to sea.'

'They're catching the last train. Do you think we could have a celebration supper? Maybe one of the girls could make a cake?'

'Celebration? I don't see any cause for that. My man's abandoned us – God knows when we'll see him again.'

Joe and Robert came in and heard this last remark. 'Don't worry, Auntie Betty, I don't want no fuss made. Ma, I'm going to pack me things.' He looked so happy. He was no longer a child, but a young man well able to take care of his own destiny.

'I'll find you a bag. Do you know what you need?'

'Uncle Robert told me.' The sound of his boots clattering on the stairs, possibly for the last time, made her blink back tears.

'I'll not be long, boys. Why don't you lay the table for Auntie Betty?' She scooped up her daughter and carried her out. 'Come along, sweetheart, you can help your big brother get his things together.'

'Where's our Joe going to, Ma? Is he going to heaven with Buster?'

'No, love, he's going with Uncle Robert to be a cabin boy on his ship. Your Uncle Alfie has gone to London to work for a while – but they will both be back one day.'

The little girl's face crumpled. 'I don't like going-away people. I want my Joe to stay here with me.'

'He's all grown up now, Mary, and has to make his own way in the world. In a year or two Davie will go and then after that it will be John's turn.'

The child sniffed loudly. 'You said that Uncle Alfie and Joe will be back by then, so I won't mind if it's Davie or John's turn.'

Her daughter hadn't quite grasped how this worked, but she was not quite three, so it was hardly surprising. She put her down and found a carpetbag tucked away at the back of her wardrobe. When she took it in to Joe he was playing hide-and-go-seek with the little one.

'Here you are. Will this be big enough?'

'I ain't taking much, Ma. We only get a locker to stow our belongings. I'm going to miss you and me brothers and sister, but I'm that excited to finally have my wish.'

'Your pa would be proud of the fine young man you've turned into. One day you will be like Robert, a captain of your own vessel.'

Joe beamed. 'I'm going to work hard, take me exams, and who knows? Don't you fret, Ma, I'll not let you down.'

She hesitated, but then hugged him and he returned the embrace. 'I'm just glad that your first berth will be with Robert. I know after this voyage you will have to take whatever's going, but by then you will be an experienced seaman.'

He pushed the items on the bed into the bag. 'There, I'm done. I ain't much for writing letters, Ma, but I'll do me best.' He straightened and touched her arm. 'I'll be here for your wedding. You deserve to be happy. You'll have me blessing when you tie the knot next year.'

'Did Robert tell you? We were going to keep it between ourselves until he got back.'

'I ain't blind. He's had a fancy for you for years. He were just waiting for you to get over my pa.' He nodded and his smile was like a blow to the chest. He looked so like Dan.

'Can I ask you to keep this to yourself? I don't want Betty upset.'

'She'll not hear nothing from me.'

4

LONDON, OCTOBER 1848

Alfie read the adverts, tramped the streets and eventually secured himself a position as a newspaper vendor on Euston Station. This was hardly a step up in the world but he needed to earn something, however meagre, if he were not to run out of money.

He had moved to a less desirable lodgings just off Tottenham Court Road, clean and such, but not as fancy as before and half the price. He had to fetch his own water and empty his own pisspot, but he weren't too proud to do that. The food were plain, but well cooked and plentiful. All in all, he were well pleased with his new drum.

He were also more comfortable mixing with the other lodgers, they were working men, with no illusions about their prospects. They were existing from one wage packet to another and content to do so. He wanted more, but for the moment would settle for regular employment, decent accommodation and living within his means.

He'd not contacted Sarah nor Betty since he'd gone down in the world – they would still think him living at the first place. With the penny post available there was no excuse for not writing again, but he couldn't bring himself to do so. If they'd replied, and he expected Sarah would have, the letter would remain unanswered.

He missed Buster something cruel, worse than when his little brother Tommy had drowned all those years ago. If there were a war on he would take the queen's shilling and become a soldier. Fighting for his country, probably dying, wouldn't be too bad.

Then, after selling newspapers outside the station for a few weeks everything changed.

He had just sold a copy of *The Times* to a smart gent in striped trousers and top hat and bid him a cheery good morning when the cry of *'stop thief'* echoed from a nearby alley. Alfie had no intention of stopping anyone, but he was interested to see who emerged. He'd been a thief himself and had sympathy for the street urchins who lived by thievery.

As expected two small, barefooted boys tore from between the houses. They both wore flapping, overlarge jackets and whatever they'd stolen must be hidden in one of the pockets. They raced past and vanished into the station. Seconds later the unmistakable sound of a police rattle joined in the general shouting.

He'd always managed to avoid being taken by a constable and this was the first time he'd seen a peeler up close. The two who appeared were red-faced and breathless from the chase. They skidded to a halt next to his news stall.

'Did you see the little buggers? They snatched the wallet of some toff and there'll be hell to pay if we ain't got them.'

Alfie was torn – the peelers looked desperate, but if they did catch the thieves they could be transported or hanged despite the fact they were children.

'I was that taken aback I scarcely noticed, Constable. I reckon they went into the station, but I ain't sure.'

The hue and cry had attracted a small crowd of passers-by and all had something to add to the conversation. Hopefully this would give the miscreants time to make their escape. The policemen shoved their way through the crowd and ran off. He could see from their dejected faces they had little expectation of being successful.

He'd make a good thief-taker, having been one of the wrongdoers himself in the past. He weren't sure what sort of candidates was wanted to join this new undertaking, but he quite fancied himself in that smart get-up. He reckoned he'd look fine in the swallowtail coat, high top hat and leather Wellington boots.

This was one avenue of employment he'd not considered – but it were a regular work, respectable like, and if he were good at his job there could be promotion. He was sure he'd seen an advert asking for suitable candidates to apply in yesterday's newspaper.

There was still a copy left somewhere at the bottom of the cart. He'd put in his penny when he'd finished in an hour or two and then find a coffee shop where he could read it in peace.

There was indeed a three-column advertisement.

> Policeman Wanted at Whitechapel Division. Active young men between twenty and thirty-five years of age, height not under 5 feet 9 inches are required in the police force. Salary 19 shillings per week.

It went on to say that testimonials of character had to be sent to the address at the bottom of the advertisement. The final day for application was today.

He only qualified on two counts – that of the height and the age but he certainly didn't have any testimonials. He reckoned he could provide his own character references. All he had to do was purchase some paper, pen and ink, and then he could write them himself.

With the necessary items he returned to his drum and took himself upstairs to the room he was obliged to share with another cove. Sid Smith were decent enough. He worked on the station doing some sort of labouring work. It were casual, no permanence, and the poor sod never knew from one week to the next if he were going to get work.

Fortunately, when he were busy he never returned until after dark, which gave Alfie the room to himself. It wouldn't do for anyone, even Sid, who were none too clever, to see him forge his testimonial.

He'd had the foresight to purchase, despite the cost, four sheets of paper as well as the envelopes, two pens and a small bottle of ink. He could write a fair hand when he set his mind to it and hoped he could get an unblemished copy from four attempts. What to put were the problem.

He recalled that Sarah had written a false reference for a friend when she was working as a nursemaid. This was what had got her dismissed when it had been discovered. She'd told him she'd just written that the girl was of good character, honest and hard-working.

He could hardly put anything truthful – the last thing the peelers wanted were candidates what had been thieves themselves. He pondered for a while and then wrote in his best script something similar to what Sarah had written for her friend. He invented a suitably impressive address and name for the person who had supposedly written this testimonial.

From what he'd learnt it were a tough life being a police constable. They worked either a night shift or day. This meant being on duty from nine at night until six in the morning or vice versa. He'd be happy to do that for nineteen shillings a week.

He waited for the ink to dry, carefully folded the first paper and pushed it into the envelope. He then addressed it as instructed and began the laborious task of writing the second certificate as to his good character. Again, he manufactured the name and gave this imaginary person an address in Chelmsford. He put them carefully into the inside pocket of his jacket. He intended to deliver the envelopes himself and not entrust them to an urchin.

The clerk he handed the letters to nodded and put them in a tray but paid him little attention. Now all he had to do was wait until the morrow when would return and fill in the necessary form and hopefully have an interview. It were customary for the testimonials to be investigated for veracity, but because he had submitted them so late he were hopeful they wouldn't bother. Of course, eventually his deception might be discovered, but not for a year or two if he were lucky.

He arrived the next morning at the designated place in good time and expected to be one of dozens hoping for appointment. In that he were mistaken as there were only him and one other cove. The man didn't look any older than him, was dressed in a similar fashion in workmen's clothes and had the look of a gypsy about him, what with his black hair and dark eyes. He wandered over and spoke to him.

'Ain't there any others applying to be constables in Whitechapel?'

'Nope, I reckon as we're the only two what applied. Ain't you heard, mister, that the constables are buggering off quicker than they can appoint fresh. It's bloody hard work, long hours for just a few shillings and somewhere to sleep.'

This was good news indeed. If they were short of applicants they were less likely to be checking his false documents. 'If that's the case, why are you here?'

'Same as you – ain't got a decent job and this will do to tide me over the winter months.' He held out his hand. 'Fred Brown.'

Alfie shook it vigorously. 'Alfie Nightingale, pleased to meet you.' They'd been left in a small, dark anteroom – the only furniture two battered, bentwood chairs. 'You got any idea what'll happen next?'

'I heard that we get examined by a surgeon, but apart from that, no idea.'

'I can hear someone coming.' Alfie turned to face the door and stood in what he hoped was a military fashion. Fred joined him. They were of equal height and build. He reckoned they'd look fine in a constable's uniform.

A clerk poked his head round the door. 'Come this way – the surgeon's ready for you now.' They followed him and he pointed to another small, dingy room. 'Remove your outer garments.' The elderly man vanished.

'I ain't got nothing wrong with me. What about you, Alfie?'

'Fit as a flea, apart from this.' He held out his damaged hand. 'I were a cabinetmaker until some bastards stamped on this. It works good enough for everything else; I just can't hold me tools. I don't reckon it'll put them off.'

A tall, middle-aged gent strolled in. He didn't introduce himself and strangely didn't ask them to identify themselves either. He gave them a cursory examination and declared they were both excellent physical specimens.

The clerk reappeared as they were scrambling back into their jackets and neckties. 'You are to fill in your details and then you will be officially appointed. Follow me.'

An hour later it were done. He were now Constable Nightingale of the

Whitechapel division. His collar number would be issued when he received his uniform the next day.

'Right, who's for a wet? It'll be the last time we can go in a beerhouse. No drinking in uniform and, as we bleeding well have to stay in that on or off-duty, let's make the most of our last night of freedom.'

Alfie was happy to let his new acquaintance take the lead. 'From what they said it's run like the military, but at least we don't get shot at.'

* * *

Chelmsford, October 1848

The house no longer seemed like home without Alfie, Joe or Buster. Sarah continued to put what she considered to be a fair wage into her personal bank account each week. As her mother owned the lease and had started the dressmaking business it was only fair she had three-quarters of the money.

Davie was already talking about leaving school. 'Ma, I ain't staying after I'm twelve. I know you and my pa wanted us to stay on until we was fourteen, but I reckon I've learnt all I'm going to already.' He held up his hand and ticked off his reasons on his fingers. 'I write a neat hand, I can figure my numbers right well, I can read anything you put in front of me. What more do I need?'

'I agree. Have you any notion what you want to do with your life?'

'I'd like to be a cabinetmaker like what Uncle Alfie was. There's a business half a mile from here. I've been speaking to the master and he'll take me on as an apprentice. It ain't cheap, mind.'

'Shall we go and see him together after school tomorrow? If I agree with you, then we will get your indentures drawn up. Will you be able to live here still or must you reside with him?'

'I don't know.'

'What would you prefer? I'd like you to stay here – I've already lost one son this year.'

'Joe ain't lost, Ma, he's gone to sea. Don't fret – you'll hear from him soon.'

She couldn't tell him it wasn't just Joe she was worried about. Robert had promised to write and have the letter conveyed back from the first ports they docked at. They had been gone almost three months, even with the vagaries of the post a letter should have arrived by now.

'I'm sure you're right, Davie. Spot is barking at the gate and John is beside himself with impatience waiting for you to take them both for their walk along the river.'

Things had also changed between her, Betty and her mother. Although Betty put on a brave face, she was quieter now and rarely smiled. Initially she had eagerly awaited the arrival of the postman but after so many weeks she no longer went to see if there was a letter for her. Her brother had promised to keep in touch, to come and visit, but for some reason he had broken his word. She prayed he hadn't fallen in with his nefarious cronies from his previous stay in the city.

Mary now spent most of her time with Sarah. She didn't want her daughter being ignored and this was what had been happening. Betty seemed to have only enough energy and interest nowadays to take care of her own two – even her housekeeping duties no longer interested her.

Ma hadn't commented on the fact that Sarah was now doing the tasks that had been designated as Betty's contribution to the household. As they employed three maids this involved little extra time on her part, as all she had to do was give instructions and then check these were carried out to her satisfaction. A local woman came in to do the heavy work and laundry, so the girls only had to press the clothes, not wash them.

She had just returned from one of her frequent visits to the bank to pay in the takings from the business and found her mother in the office going through the account books. Sarah had been quite open about the money she was taking but she hadn't brought it to Ma's attention, not wanting there to be any confrontation.

'Helping yourself to my money, are you then?'

'No, Ma, I'm paying myself a reasonable wage for the work I do here. You will note that I've deducted two pounds every week to cover board and lodging for my family.'

From the sour expression on her parent's face this information had already been noted and hadn't ameliorated her disapproval. 'I took you and your children into my home from the goodness of my heart. I didn't expect you to steal from me...'

'Ma, that's quite enough of that sort of talk. You know as well as I do that we would not be making as much money if I was not here to run the business and design the garments. You were making a fraction of what you are now when we came two years ago. Have you checked the balance of your account?'

'I was about to do that when I saw what you've been up to.'

'I've been up to nothing untoward. You would have to pay twice as much as I'm taking if I wasn't here.' She had intended to stop there but her anxiety about the missing members of her family caused her to speak more harshly than was sensible. 'What would your friends at church think about a mother and grandmother behaving as you are doing? You abandoned us when we needed you. Leaving me a golden guinea and six handkerchiefs was hardly compensation for what you took away.'

She had her mother's full attention now. Her expression was less hostile.

'I was devastated when I came back to visit and found you had gone without saying goodbye or leaving a forwarding address. You know what happened to me, what happened to Alfie, and yet you begrudge our very existence in your house.'

'Sarah love, I'm sorry to have spoken to you so harshly. You're right to take me to task. I never thought to see you again and yet now I have three wonderful grandchildren.'

The omission of Joe, Davie and John did not go unnoticed, but at least the frigid atmosphere was gone.

'Of course, you must take your share of the profits – you deserve it. I've not been myself since Alfie left. The house doesn't seem right without a man in it. I know he didn't feel comfortable not bringing in a wage, but I was that proud of him, I didn't care.'

If only Ma had said this to him before he'd decided he wasn't wanted.

'I'm sorry too, Ma. We mustn't fall out. We're family and we should support and love each other no matter what. I just wish Alfie and Joe would write to us so we know they're well.'

'Betty's miserable – scarcely get a word out of her nowadays. Why don't you fetch her in, ring for a nice pot of tea and some of the fruit cake? We'll have a chat about things and clear the air.'

Betty was fetched and whilst the three younger children played quietly on the floor the three of them talked – something they should have done weeks ago.

5

WHITECHAPEL, LONDON

Alfie reported the next morning at the new station house situated at 37 to 39 Leman Street. He was sent immediately to collect his uniform from the storekeeper housed at the rear of the fine new building. With his large parcel under one arm, and his carpetbag in the other hand, he went in search of his accommodation in the section house at 26 Leman Street.

The row of small, terraced houses had been rented by the Metropolitan authority solely for the purpose of housing police constables.

The cottage consisted of two rooms upstairs and two down. The front door opened into the only parlour, sparsely furnished with four wooden chairs, a table, a bookshelf and a fireplace with coal scuttle and necessary implements. There weren't even a rag rug to cheer the place up.

He pushed open the door on the far side and saw it led into a small kitchen and scullery, which was also used as the washroom. From the look of it no one did much cooking, but there were clean water waiting in the china jugs. He glanced out of the small window and saw the yard was shared by the other dozen cottages. There were only four privies – better than it might have been.

He'd been informed that he would be sharing with the three other men who he would be on duty with. He would be expected to work from six in the morning until nine at night if he was on day shift and then four others would relieve him and his colleagues whenever his allocated period had expired.

As he returned to the front room Fred stepped in. His new friend looked around. 'Blimey, this ain't too grand, is it?'

'I've lived in worse and at least it only costs us a shilling a week from our wages. I ain't been upstairs as yet – shall we see what's what?'

In order to access the stairs you opened the door in the wall. The steps were steep and their boots clattered on the wooden treads. There was no landing – just a square about a yard wide and two doors facing each other.

'This one's taken; the other must be ours. Bugger me! Hardly room to swing a cat in here.'

Fred pulled a face as he dumped his bag and parcel on the bed nearest the door. 'I wasn't expecting much, but this ain't much better than a drum in the Rookeries.'

'It's clean enough, but it'll be perishing in the winter. I reckon we'll have to purchase extra bedding, if it's allowed. There ain't no cupboards; there's the shelf and a couple of hooks. We'll have to make do with them.'

It didn't take them long to unpack their few personal items. Alfie had wisely disposed of the remaining paper, pen and ink before he'd left his lodgings. He carefully unwrapped the brown paper parcel to expose the clothes he would be obliged to wear in future at all times. Even when he was off-duty he had to wear them. There was a cloth cuff to put on his left wrist to indicate when he weren't working.

They examined their uniforms in silence. 'I reckon this coat will fit me well enough, and the shirt and trousers.' He held up the swallowtail jacket with shiny buttons. 'Look here, we've got a number each on the collar.'

'These are the winter trousers – going to be a bit hot until the weather changes. We've even got a greatcoat – I ain't sure why it's brown instead of blue like the rest – and there's a cape for when it's raining.'

They shed their ordinary clothes and dressed for the first time as constables. The leather boots was a bit loose but better that than too tight. What neither of them liked were the bloody great belt, four inches broad with a great buckle some six inches deep.

Alfie was ready first and picked up the rabbit-skin, high top hat. It fitted a treat and apart from the thick leather stock that were choking him, he reckoned he would do all right.

Suitably attired they made the short walk to the police station where the sergeant on duty was to give them their instructions. There weren't time to stop for a bite to eat; he hoped he'd get a chance to grab something from a coffee stall later on.

Sergeant Kavanagh was waiting for them. He seemed a jovial sort of cove, a head shorter than both he and Fred, a bald pate and a fierce, ginger moustache.

'I'll take you around your beat and point out important landmarks. You patrol two and a half miles and will walk around twenty miles each beat. You are strictly forbidden to lean on anything or to sit down. You will be working seven days a week. Unfortunately, you are not entitled to any refreshment breaks or hot meals. You must use your initiative where these are concerned.'

It were going to be harder than he'd thought, better than being unemployed, but only just. He were earning five times his current weekly wage when he were a cabinetmaker but no point in repining – he were lucky to have a roof over his head in the circumstances.

The sergeant pointed to the noticeboard upon which were pinned several sheets of printed paper. 'These are the rules and regulations that you are expected to adhere to at all times. You must peruse them in your own time and be ready to answer speedily if you are questioned by an inspector.'

He nodded but offered no response.

'The most important of these rules is that you must not get drunk, must remain respectable at all times. Stick to that and you'll do all right, lads.'

There was no time to discuss any of this with Fred as they were marched out onto the street. Kavanagh now had on his own top hat and Alfie reckoned no one would recognise him, not even his own family, dressed as he was.

They walked at a steady pace, he and Fred abreast and Sergeant Kavanagh one step in front. This was familiar territory to him, north along the City of London boundary line to Hackney Road, then east to White

Street, south through Charles Street and into New Road and on to Cannon Street Road, then Old Gravel Lane on the riverside at Wapping. They then trudged westwards to the Tower of London and back along the city boundary.

In a full shift they would cover this beat eight times – unless something untoward took place and they had to deal with that. After they had completed two circuits the sergeant halted outside the police station.

'Righto, lads, you know the drill. Continue to cover your beat, prevent pilfering and any other crime you come across. From tomorrow you will patrol separately. You must walk at a steady pace. In this manner the villains in the area are aware a policeman will be coming past every quarter of an hour.'

'Yes, sir, we understand.' Fred spoke for the both of them.

The remainder of their shift was uneventful. Not even an altercation, or an urchin stealing from a market stall, to alleviate the boredom of marching around the same streets.

'Here, Fred, no one has explained to us exactly what to do to arrest a villain. Can we thump the bugger?'

'Reckon so. We've got that loop of rope and toggle thing to put around their wrists to restrain them, but damned if I know what else we're supposed to do.'

'We need to talk to the other two in our relief; they'll be able to put us straight. We have to do nights, but Gawd knows when. I reckon it'll be a mite more interesting at night.'

'We've got to write down everything what happens in our little books. At least today we ain't got nothing to put down.'

***

Chelmsford, November 1848

There had still been no word from Alfie but that morning she had received five letters, which arrived together, two from Robert and three from Joe. The delay in their arrival was to do with the transport they had been placed on. Both Robert and Joe were perfectly well. She opened one from her fiancé first.

Dearest Sarah,

I cannot tell you what joy it gives me to be able to address you as my love. Joe has settled in well and has the makings of an excellent seaman. He suffered not at all from seasickness and is eager to learn everything about his new life.

The further we sail from England the more I think about you. The sea is my life, but I believe if you truly wish me to, I could give it up for you.

I hope you have also heard from Alfie. I can understand his reason for leaving but if he does not contact Betty that would be reprehensible of him.

There is nothing much of interest to report. The weather is remarkably clement and we are making good speed towards our first port of call in Africa.

I shall post this missive when we dock. I shall write again and although you cannot respond I know that you hold me in your heart as I do you in mine,

Your loving Robert

She held the paper to her nose and was sure she could detect the faint aroma of the sea.

'Ma, Ma, Grandma says you're to come to the shop and speak to a customer.' Mary tugged at her skirt to get her attention.

'I'm coming, love, I've just received letters from Uncle Robert and your big brother. I've yet to open the ones from Joe. We shall do it together later.'

Her daughter was approaching her third birthday and was already attracting the attention of the customers with her charm and prettiness. She was as great a favourite with the seamstresses as she was with their clients. This was why Ma insisted the little girl spent as much time as possible in the shop.

Yet another reason for Betty to feel slighted. Her friend was now resigned to the fact that she was without her husband and was making the best of it. However, she was doing less towards the running of the household and spending the majority of her time with her children who were thriving with so much attention.

So far there was no sign that Betty was looking for physical comfort elsewhere – indeed, she had made it abundantly clear when approached by a gentleman, after a visit to a concert, that she was a married woman and he was to keep his suggestions to himself.

The customer wanted an entire wardrobe for herself and her small daughter. The order was the best they'd had this year and would put several pounds into her growing savings. By the time the woman had settled on fabrics and designs the boys were home from school.

Davie was working for a few hours each day with the cabinetmaker and would start his apprenticeship full-time when he left school at the end of the Michaelmas term. As long as he was at his place of work by seven o'clock every morning his master was content to have her son remain at home.

'Boys, it will be your sister's birthday in three weeks' time. I thought we could have a party to celebrate – it is far too long since we did anything of this sort.'

'That'll be grand, Ma. I've been making her a crib and one of them little chairs, like what Uncle Alfie made for her when she was small, but tiny like to fit her dolly, and they'll be done by then.'

'I hope you got permission.'

He grinned. 'Not only that, his missus has asked me to make one of each for her kiddies for their Christmas gift.'

'That's wonderful. I know you're making Tommy and Jimmy a train set. I'm not surprised you've been so eager to go every afternoon.'

He gobbled down sandwiches and soup, changed into something more serviceable, and was eager to leave.

'Would you mind if we walked with you? I thought to order something pretty for Betty and your grandma.'

John, as always, had rushed off to take Spot for a long ramble along the riverbank. Betty had gone visiting with her children and she was not required in the shop or workroom this afternoon. Her office duties were completed so she was free to do as she pleased.

Mary was dancing from foot to foot at this unexpected treat. 'I've not seen where you work, Davie. Thank you for taking me.'

Sarah hesitated at the front door, considering whether to take her umbrella. It had been the wettest year she could remember but for once the sky was clear of black clouds, even if it was decidedly chilly.

Davie walked proudly at her side. He was growing up so fast and was, like Joe, going to be taller than her before long. Mary held on to her brother's hand, skipping along, talking non-stop, and several people turned to watch her and smile in appreciation.

It wasn't far to the cabinetmaker's premises. 'Here, Mary, take Ma's hand now. I've got to go on ahead and make sure I'm allowed to bring you in.' He winked at Sarah and she understood immediately. He wanted to hide the gifts he was making for his little sister.

'You must promise to be a good girl, Mary. There are lots of sharp things that could hurt you. You must keep hold of my hand.'

'I will, I will. Davie's looking round the door and beckoning to us. Can we run?'

Sarah picked up her skirts before answering. 'We certainly can, sweetheart. See who can get there first.'

Her son scooped up her daughter when she arrived squealing with laughter. 'My, what a fast runner you are. Ma wants to speak to the master so you come with me and I'll show you everything. You mustn't touch, mind.'

The large workshop was well organised, plenty of room for the proprietor, the foreman and senior cabinetmaker, plus the three apprentices, to work without getting in each other's way. Immediately she was reminded of her brother – where was he? Why hadn't he sent them a communication of some sort? She rubbed the moisture from her eyes with her gloved hand.

Mr Cox, the owner, wiped his hands on his apron and came over to greet her with a smile. 'Mrs Cooper, I am delighted to meet you. Your Davie is a credit to you. He's a hard worker and has a talent for carpentry. He tells me his uncle was a cabinetmaker too?'

'He was, Mr Cox, but unfortunately he injured his right hand and was no longer able to ply his trade. Thank you for your compliments, and I thank you for taking him in so readily. He cannot wait to start working here full-time in the new year.'

'I have something for you, Mrs Cooper, if you would care to come into my office.'

She followed him into what was presumably part of his dwelling. He gestured towards one of the chairs by his desk and she took her place.

'Your boy made me one of the baby chairs that his uncle designed. I cannot think why more of them are not made. Adding a padded cushion to the seat makes them safer and more comfortable for the little ones. I have already sold more than a dozen and have orders for a dozen more.'

'I'm delighted to hear that. Davie told me he's making miniatures of the crib and baby chair I had for his sister as gifts for her birthday and Christmas.'

'He's got a natural talent for miniatures, Mrs Cooper. He can learn his trade making them the same as he can doing items of a normal size.' He pulled out a drawer and removed a small leather bag. 'This is for your boy. I put by a threepence for every chair I've made from his design.'

'You should give it to him yourself – he will be overjoyed by your generosity.'

'I have no wish to play favourites in front of the other apprentices. He has settled in well, but even a blind man could not fail to see he has more aptitude than the other two of them put together.'

She picked up the purse and put it in her bag. 'Thank you, Mr Cox. I can assure you he'll not talk about this here. I came to see if you had anything already made that might do for gifts for my mother and my sister-in-law.'

He showed her some pretty inlaid boxes that had been made for a wealthy gentleman who had since died and his family had declined to honour the order. She chose two and left well satisfied with her visit.

'Why isn't Davie coming back with us, Ma?'

'He has to work until six o'clock, my love, but he will be home in time for supper as always. We must hurry back because I've not yet read your brother Joe's letters. Shall we run a little?'

Although they always departed through the front door but returned via the side gate as this did not necessitate calling one of the girls away from more important duties in order to open the door. No sooner had she stepped into the house than she detected something had changed – and it wasn't for the better.

Her heart sank to her boots. It was as if she had swallowed a large stone and it had settled in her stomach. Instinctively she gathered her daughter into her arms.

Betty had been waiting for her in the office and put her finger to her lips, then indicated they should creep through the house and go upstairs. Sarah's heart began to return to its usual pace. There had not been bad news, nobody had died, but there was definitely something wrong.

As she scurried up the stairs with Mary still in her arms she could hear Tommy and Jimmy playing in their bedroom. 'Run along, sweetheart – go and play with your cousins. No arguing and keep the baby safe.'

'I can do that, Ma. I'm a big girl now.'

Betty had retreated into the room she had once shared with Alfie. Sarah hurried to join her.

'That bastard Hatch has found us, Sarah. He turned up half an hour ago looking for my Alfie.'

6

'I suppose it was inevitable he would find us eventually. Thank God Alfie isn't living here – I shudder to think what would happen if he was. It might well end up in murder, either his or Hatch's.'

'I was walking back along the other side of the road when I saw him and two of his men heading for the shop. I waited until he was inside and then nipped in the back and hid up here.' Betty was more animated than she had been for months.

'I think it best if we remain where we are until he's gone. Ma has only to speak the truth: Alfie's not living here and we have no idea where he is. This is the first time I've been glad my brother hasn't written since that first note he sent a few weeks after he left.'

'I do miss him something cruel, but I'm learning to get on without him. At least I have a roof over my head, my children are happy and I don't have to have a baby every year.'

Sarah nodded her agreement. 'I was fortunate I didn't catch on again before Dan died. Being a respectable married woman, or widow in my case, has many advantages over the single state. God knows why men think we are capable of running a business once we have a ring on our fingers but cannot be trusted to do so before we're married.'

'My Alfie will come back one day and I'll be happy to have another little one then as these two will be independent. Will you ever get married again? That Robert has taken a shine to you.'

She was about to reveal her secret to Betty when her mother called up the stairs. 'He's gone. It's safe to come down now.'

'What did he want? What did you tell him, Ma?'

'That I've not seen Alfie since the summer, have no idea where he is, that he has abandoned his family and gone to London to start a new life.'

'Did he believe you?'

'I think so. It's hard to credit he's such a villain. He was perfectly pleasant to me. I had tea fetched into the parlour and he told me he was recently widowed.'

Betty joined them and heard this last remark. 'He can be charming when he wishes, Ma. Don't be fooled by him – he's bad through and through.' She put Jimmy down on the floor to crawl about and laughed – not something she did much of lately. 'Be careful he doesn't set his cap at you, Ma. A wealthy independent widow would suit him just fine.'

The three of them laughed at the thought and conversation turned to other things until Davie burst in.

'I saw that bastard Hatch walk past the workshop just as I was leaving. I followed him and he got on the train. Has he been bothering you, Ma?'

'I didn't speak to him, son, but your grandma sent him packing. He knows your uncle no longer lives here and that should be enough for him.'

'I ain't so sure. If that were the case why's he left his two bully boys watching the house?'

Sarah's instinct was to go and look through the window but she restrained herself. She took a steadying breath before she answered. 'I expect he wishes to be certain Alfie isn't just out for the day. I imagine they will hang about for a few days, make enquiries with our neighbours, and then will be satisfied that your grandmother was telling the truth.'

John sidled closer, his face anxious. 'Why does he want to find Uncle Alfie?'

'They have unfinished business, love – nothing for any of us to worry about. I doubt we'll see him again as he has his business interests in Colchester and we have ours in Chelmsford.'

She prayed she was speaking the truth, that her words were not empty ones, for she had a nasty feeling Hatch intended to disrupt her well-ordered life. If he couldn't get his revenge on her brother then he was the sort of man who would vent his anger on his family instead.

That night she found it difficult to sleep as her head was full of unpleasant possibilities. How could he damage them? They were secure financially, thank the good Lord for that. Never again would she and her family be destitute and forced to rely on the goodwill of others.

The three maids lived in. They had a room in the attic, and she heard them going down to the kitchen to get the bread kneaded and put on the back of the range to rise so it could be baked fresh for breakfast. She would go down to the office and read the other letters she had received yesterday. This would occupy her time nicely until her daughter woke up and needed her attention.

Joe told her in his first letter, a very short one, that he was loving his work and had made the right choice of career. He promised to write again soon. She opened the second, little more than a few words scrawled on a piece of paper. Again, it said little about his life apart from the fact he was happy.

She spent longer perusing Robert's missives. He too wrote little about his daily life, the exotic sights he was seeing, just repeated the same sentiments he had stressed in his first one. She was vaguely disappointed. She had not thought him a dull man, had expected to be given vivid descriptions, exciting anecdotes of his life aboard a trading vessel – instead his letters were loving, affectionate, but no more than that.

Had she made an error of judgement in agreeing to marry him? Then her lips curved as she recalled his embrace before he'd left. He might be a man of few words, but he was passionate and that would do her very well.

When they married she intended to continue working, to build her own business making clothes for women and children. She had no wish for him to give up his life on the ship – having him away for months and then home for a few weeks would suit her very well. She had become an independent woman since her beloved Dan had died and had no wish to return to being only a wife and mother.

They had the rest of their lives to get to know each other better. Had he not come to her rescue on more than one occasion but always behaved as the perfect gentleman towards her? Being married to a ship's captain would give her prestige amongst her clientele but still allow her the freedom to be herself, as well as the best wife she could be. She was determined that when Robert was home on leave she would devote her entire attention to him, but when he was gone she would resume her enterprise.

* * *

Whitechapel, London, December 1848

The first two weeks of his life as a police constable Alfie reckoned were almost as hard as when he was enslaved on a coal lighter shovelling for hours on end. The weather was miserable and on more than one occasion he was soaked through even with his sturdy cape on. He had no access to dry garments and was obliged to conduct his duty as he was.

The other two constables who made up his relief had been employed only a few months and yet were already discussing handing in their notice as they found their duties too onerous. Fred and he had become good mates and Alfie had told him a little of his life.

'Married with two nippers? Well I never! From what you says, Alfie, you had a comfortable billet – I'd jump at the chance of being kept in luxury with nothing more to do than stroll about the place.'

'I were stupid to leave. I miss me wife and children – I reckon I'll go down and see them tomorrow. We're going on nights so I'll have the day free. If I catch the first train, I'll have plenty of time for a visit. It's me niece's birthday next week.'

'It wouldn't be so bad if I'd had more to do than arrest a couple of pickpockets, help put out a fire, and stop a couple of fights outside a beerhouse,' Fred said.

'I ain't had much more excitement. I reckon there's more doing at night when the burglaries take place. At least we've found ourselves a coffee stall so we can get a hot drink and something to eat during the day.'

* * *

Alfie was up at dawn. He dressed quickly. It were damn cold upstairs with ice on the inside of the window of his bedroom. The four of them who lived in this cottage were all transferring to night duty so no one had to get up early today apart from himself who was catching a train from Liverpool Street Station.

He weren't supposed to wear his own clothes, but he weren't going to travel in his uniform. He hadn't decided whether to tell his family about his new occupation. His wallet was satisfactorily full and he intended to give Betty a substantial sum to buy herself and the kiddies something nice for Christmas. He still had an envelope and he put four ten-bob notes into it. He then wrote a quick note.

Betty love,

I'm sorry that I left and if you'll have me back I'll come. I should never have gone. I miss you and the kiddies and if you let me return I'll promise to be a better husband and father. Buy yourself and the boys something nice.

Your Alfie

Apart from the one letter he'd sent a few weeks after his arrival in London he'd not communicated and he were ashamed. It would serve him right if Betty had looked elsewhere – he were no sort of husband to her. He stepped off the train feeling happy for the first time in months. Depending on his reception, he might give in his notice and come home and make the best of what he had.

What Fred had said had opened Alfie's eyes to his stupidity. He should've been grateful to have a good roof over his head and a pretty, loving wife and two sons – not to mention Sarah and her family, and his ma. He was about to leave the station precinct when a guard hurried up to him. He hoped today's visit, and his gift, might help her to forgive him.

'Excuse me, are you Alfie Nightingale?'

'What's it to you, mister?'

'Quick, come with me. There's a man called Hatch looking for you and he's left two of his men to see if you turn up.'

Alfie didn't ask how the guard knew all this. He were just relieved to be tipped the wink. 'I'm grateful for your warning. When's the next train back?'

'Half an hour. You can hide in here – no one comes in this storeroom except me.'

'Will you get a message to me missus?' He reached into his pocket and brought out the envelope. 'Do you have a pencil I could borrow?'

The guard handed Alfie a small stub of a thing, but it had a point and would serve the purpose. He scribbled on the back of the envelope.

Betty love,

I just heard that bastard Hatch has found you. I were coming back, but I ain't going to now. I'm not bringing trouble on your head. Take care of yourself and the boys.

Your Alfie

He shoved the envelope into the man's hand and stepped into the storeroom, not wishing his misery to be seen. He hadn't realised until this moment how much he wanted to come home and now he never could. He couldn't provide his family with anything like the luxury they now enjoyed. The best he could offer, if he were lucky, were accommodation in married quarters, which wouldn't be much better than what he had now.

No, better for everyone that he stayed away.

On the train back to the city his misery turned to anger. Why should he be driven from his family because of that evil bastard? He were a peeler now – if he could get a good name maybe in a few months he could hand in his notice and get a transfer to Chelmsford. With the law on his side he reckoned he could find some excuse to arrest Hatch...

No sooner had he thought this than he understood it could never happen. Hatch would reveal Alfie's nefarious past and not only would he lose his position he might end up being transported or dancing at the end of a rope.

He could see only one way he could ever return to his family and that was if he murdered Hatch. Despite his anguish he smiled. Hardly a suitable thought for a member of the Metropolitan Police.

* * *

Chelmsford, December 1848

It would be Mary's anniversary soon and Sarah wanted to hold a party. She supposed she would have to get her mother's permission as legally the roof over their head belonged to her or at least the lease did. Business had been booming as the womenfolk wanted a new gown for themselves and garments for their children in time for the Christmas celebrations.

The weather had improved and over the past few weeks they had been obliged to take on two extra seamstresses. Her mother started to go out every week, dressed in her finest, ostensibly to meet up with some of her friends. It was a mystery to her and Betty why it was necessary to look so smart when just visiting friends.

She went in search of her mother and found her, as was often the case nowadays, perusing the books in the office. This was no longer solely Sarah's domain and this made her a little uncomfortable.

'Ma, I intend to hold a party for Mary. The little ones have never had a party – in fact there hasn't been one since Dan died.'

Her mother looked up from column of figures she was studying. 'I've no objection, Sarah, as long as it's only family. I find I can't abide other people's children.'

This was an odd thing to say as the shop was often full of their clients' offspring who had come to try on the ready-made clothes on offer.

'As we don't know anyone here very well it will only be family. I had no idea you felt so strongly about young ones.'

'I'm too old to be pestered by those who are not related to me.' Her mother stopped and flushed painfully. 'Of course, I'm not referring to your stepsons.'

'Good gracious, Ma, you can't be more than forty years of age – I have a friend in Colchester who had a baby at that age.' Talking about Ada Billings made her wish she could invite the whole tribe of them. It would be a pleasure to see them and to be able to talk about Robert.

'As I am a widow with no prospect of marrying again, thankfully I do not have that concern.' She patted the book with more affection than she showed the family pet. 'Things are going very well. I would like to take on more private clients and have you design especially for them.'

'That's not what we started this business for, Ma. I agreed to make a fresh wardrobe for Mrs Mayhew as she's a personal friend of yours. I've no intention of doing it for anyone else. We cannot compete with the London fashion houses and those sorts of clients are demanding and more likely to refuse to pay their accounts.'

This did not go down well. Her mother's expression changed and she stared at Sarah almost as if she didn't like what she saw. A flicker of unease ran down her back.

'I see. I had hoped you would support me in my desire to improve the business. I had thought to look for bigger premises, then the shop and sewing rooms could be incorporated into the house to give us an excellent drawing room. I'm looking into having an indoor privy – perhaps a separate room for bathing with its own water supply.'

If she had announced she was going to see the queen, Sarah could not have been more astonished by this announcement. They already employed three servants, two more than was necessary, they had water that could be accessed in the scullery by the use of the pump and as much hot water as they needed from the boiler. Indoor plumbing was a luxury she had never encountered and had not thought to experience herself.

Her hesitation was noted and her mother frowned.

'I think that's an exciting proposition. Will it not be expensive to install such wonders in so old a house?'

'I'm having plans drawn up and the builder and engineer have assured me it will not be prohibitive. My friend already has a bathroom and flushing WC in the house. I cannot possibly invite her here until I can provide her with the same facilities. Imagine their horror if they were obliged to use our primitive arrangement outside.'

'As I have not met the lady in question, I am unable to comment on that. I should love to meet her – perhaps I could come with you next time you go? Has she frequented our humble establishment?'

'She has not. I met her when I joined the Chelmsford Women's Guild. Mrs Forsyth is our most prominent member and I am honoured to have been singled out to be her confidante.'

'To look at you now, Ma, one would not know you were not a member of the gentility. I think that the entire family has gone up in the world these past two years. Being dressed so well and living in such a comfortable abode has given us a position in the town.'

It occurred to Sarah that permission would have to be obtained from the owners of the building as Ma only had a lease. It was none of her business, so she would not enquire further.

Her mother was called to attend to a customer who refused to be served by anyone but herself. She had not answered Sarah's question and this had been a deliberate omission. For some reason Ma didn't wish her to meet her smart friend and she could think of no valid reason why this should be so. This was a mystery that she was determined to solve.

Before she went in search of Betty she looked at the same column of figures her mother had been staring at. This was the day journal, the ledger in which she recorded the takings each night. There was another book for expenses and the two were reconciled at the end of every week. The petty cash was then replenished so Betty had sufficient for day-to-day expenses and then the remainder was banked. A proportion into her own account and the rest to her mother.

Her friend was in the parlour teaching Mary and Tommy their letters whilst Jimmy played on the rug with his wooden bricks.

'Betty, do you know anything about a Mrs Forsyth? Also, were you aware my mother intended to install indoor plumbing and an actual bathroom with running water?'

'I did know about the plumbing and assumed that you did too. They had a flushing lavatory at the Saracens – it was a marvel. Imagine having no po under the bed – I never imagined living in such luxury. I wish my Alfie could come back and share it with us.'

'We can afford it, or I should say that my mother can afford it as she seems to think the business is entirely hers and I am just an employee.'

'What does that make me then? Little more than an upper servant, half housekeeper and half nanny.' This was comment was accompanied by a wry smile. Lately, she had been really enjoying the company of her friend once more, who now appeared to be resigned to her false widowhood.

'What about this Mrs Forsyth? I've never heard of her, but then I don't mix in the same grand circles as my mother appears to do.'

'I'll make enquiries next time I visit Nancy. She's an inveterate gossip and knows everyone and everything that goes on in this town.' Betty sighed and pulled a face. 'To be honest I've never really felt at home in Chelmsford. I much prefer Colchester, more going on there and there's a livelier atmosphere.'

This was the perfect opportunity to tell her friend about her plans to marry Robert. She was about to do so when the door burst open and Davie appeared. His expression was grim as he handed Betty an envelope.

7

WHITECHAPEL, DECEMBER 1848

Alfie had recovered his temper by the time he got back to his cottage. He hastily changed into his uniform, remembering to put on the band around his left cuff to indicate he wasn't on duty, and went in search of a hot meal.

There was a pie shop on his beat that he frequented and he headed there. When he was replete he decided to go to the Tower where there was some sort of do on today. He didn't want to return to his miserable lodgings until a few hours before he was due on duty. He would catch a couple of hours' kip and then his relief had to present themselves at the station house and from there they would be solemnly marched by the sergeant to where their duty started.

There was a fine old racket going on, marching bands, stilt-walkers, men bowling up and down on the newfangled penny-farthing bike, and even a couple of fire-eaters to entertain the gullible crowds. He remained on the outside of the crowd and was watching the antics of two clowns when his eye was drawn to a young man dressed as a country bumpkin.

There was something about him what didn't sit right. He weren't sure what, but he moved closer to observe the so-called countryman's actions. As he watched, the man dipped into the pocket of a wealthy gentleman and removed something, the silk of the handkerchief quite clear as he stuffed it into his inside pocket, and then he moved on to the next gullible mark. These fetched a pretty penny as he well knew from his time as a pickpocket, what seemed now like two lifetimes ago.

Without conscious thought he stepped forward and seized the culprit. The handcuffs were already out and he slipped them over the man's wrist and pulled the toggle to tighten them. He had no need to get out his wooden truncheon from the pocket in the tail of his coat.

'Come along with me, you villain. Your thieving days are over.'

The man swore and struggled, much to the amusement of the crowd but Alfie was stronger and determined to march his first arrest back to Leman Street. He was surprised the thief hadn't taken better care when there was a peeler in the vicinity. It weren't as if with his height and his top hat he weren't easy to spot.

He took the man to the front desk, which was usually manned by the sergeant on duty. This afternoon Inspector Burgess was doing this task.

'I've arrested this man as he were perpetrating a crime, that of stealing a silk handkerchief.'

'Well done, Constable. I've not had the pleasure of meeting you before. Are you a new recruit?'

'I joined a few weeks back, sir. Constable Nightingale – privileged to make your acquaintance.'

Alfie had been shown the procedure involved when bringing in a villain but this was the first time he'd actually come in with anyone who needed processing. Inspector Burgess noticed his hesitation and chuckled.

'Right, Nightingale, we shall take this thief into an interview room. There you will search him, record what you find from his person, and then formally arrest him for his crimes.'

The search revealed half a dozen men's handkerchiefs, and two dainty white lace squares from a lady. With a few gentle prompts from his superior he completed the necessary paperwork and a constable took the miserable fellow to the cells. The miscreant would be taken before the magistrate the next morning and no doubt given a heavy sentence for his crimes.

Unfortunately, he would be required to accompany the prisoner and give his statement to the magistrate. This would have to be done after tramping around Whitechapel all night.

The inspector was a jovial fellow and seemed much taken with him. 'Damn good show, Constable Nightingale. I'm impressed with your diligence. Would you be prepared to undertake some undercover work in the near future?'

Alfie wasn't sure what this meant but didn't want to show his ignorance. 'I ain't available at night, sir, but would be happy to help in the day as long as I get a few hours' shut-eye.'

'Good man. You are exactly the sort of person I've been looking for – someone who shows initiative and isn't afraid of hard work.'

Alfie touched his hat and marched out soldier-straight and pleased with his performance. Catching the notice of a senior officer were an excellent thing. He would have to ask around, discreetly like, and discover exactly what 'undercover' work entailed.

He stopped for a coffee and bun before returning to his lodgings. It were now after one o'clock, plenty of time to catch a few hours' sleep before his first night shift.

* * *

Fred, Alfie and the two other members of their relief were marched to their starting point. They were told that night duty was no different from the day, apart from the fact they were likely to be busier. The majority of serious crime took place under cover of darkness.

'Be aware, constables, that your London cracksman is more like to have the look of a sharp businessman. From their superior manner and dress it is hard to detect their real character. One might pass one daily in the street and not be able to recognise them. I advise you to be vigilant but do not interfere with the lawful passage of genuine toffs.'

With this conflicting advice ringing in his ears, Alfie set off in the darkness. Most of the streets were lit by gas lamps but the gaps between each was dark and could hold any number of lurking dangers. He preferred the night-time. The more collars he made the quicker he'd get his promotion. If he couldn't go home then he must make himself a respectable life in the police force.

He was walking past a smart residence when a slight noise on the roof attracted his attention. To his astonishment he saw two well-dressed men climbing along the tiles. He had been walking in the shadows and was certain he was unobserved.

Should he get out his rattle and try and bring assistance, or attempt to apprehend the burglars himself? He decided on the latter. He ran silently in the shadow of the houses, keeping a keen ear to what was going on above him. He followed them until they vanished through a window into an empty house, but he were unsure exactly which one it were. There was no lights in any of the buildings and he were loath to bang on any doors.

Eventually he found an unoccupied building and thundered up the stairs. He was too late. He could see where they had climbed in through an attic window but they were long gone. He was about to trudge back disappointed when something caught his eye on the sloping roof of the adjacent building.

He leant further out and saw it were a top hat – it must have blown from one of the heads of the escaping villains and landed in a place they could not access. However, he could do so and this would be a valuable piece of evidence.

There was a light in the basement kitchen and he knocked smartly on the door. It was opened by a boy. 'I am Constable Nightingale. There is a hat dropped by a burglar upon your roof. I should like to recover it.'

'Help yourself, mister. I'll show you the backstairs so you won't wake up the master and mistress with your clumping boots.'

A quarter of an hour later, the object safely under his arm, he tossed the helpful child a penny and returned to the empty street. Presumably, in the circumstances, it would be permissible to abandon his beat and return to the police station to report the crime and hand in the evidence.

He stopped in a flickering pool of yellow light thrown down from a lamp post to examine his find. To his delight he saw the item had recently been repaired and there was a slip of paper tucked inside the lining inscribed with the owner's name.

When he reached the entrance to Leman Street Station he marched in and straight to the custody desk. He explained the reason for abandoning his duties.

'Show me, Constable Nightingale. Let me read the slip of paper for myself.' The sergeant examined it and nodded. 'We have been trying to apprehend this villain for months, but he is a slippery customer and nothing ever sticks. Now we have clear evidence of his wrongdoing.'

'The house they burgled were empty, sir. I knocked to make sure when I passed a second time. I saw the two of them come out of the skylight and they came back through the attic of another unoccupied building.'

'There's nothing more you can do tonight. Fill in your pocketbook with the details and then return to your patrol. Be assured I shall mention your good work to Inspector Burgess. He has asked me to keep an eye on you.'

* * *

Chelmsford, December 1848

'My friend at the station gave me this for you, Auntie Betty. It's from Uncle Alfie,' Davie said as he handed over a crumpled letter.

Betty read the note scrawled on the back of the envelope and her hand flew to her mouth. 'He's not coming back, not ever, not now that Hatch knows where we live.' She gulped, dropped the envelope and ran out, leaving an uncomfortable silence behind.

Davie dropped to his knees and started to play a lively game with the three children and they immediately forgot Betty's distress. Sarah picked up the discarded letter and read what her brother had said for herself. There was something inside the envelope and Betty hadn't waited to open it.

She looked inside and saw there was a second note and four ten-shilling notes. When she read this her eyes brimmed. He had intended to visit, had come especially for his niece's birthday, but had changed his plans when told about Hatch and the unpleasant thugs he had left to watch their home.

'Davie, can you watch the children for a little while? I need to speak to your Auntie Betty and show her what else was in the envelope.'

'No trouble at all, Ma – nothing I like better than playing with the little ones. Our John should be in here too. He's spending too much time wandering about on his own getting into mischief after school.'

'I know. I've been distracted lately but will speak to him tonight. We need to stick together at a time like this.'

Davie looked troubled. 'Why ain't we heard again from Joe? It's weeks since we had his last letters.'

'Remember that I told you there's no actual post service from abroad. The letters have to be given to a sailor on a ship that's coming back to England and there's no guarantee they will bother to post them on. They could just toss them over the side and keep the money they were given.'

'Right enough, I'll stop worrying. It's a long way to India. He could be gone for more than a year, maybe even two.'

'Let's hope not. Now be good, children, and I'll be back soon.'

Her friend was sitting on her bed crying into an already sodden handkerchief. 'There's no need to get in such a state, Betty. There was another note and some money inside the envelope that you didn't see.'

'I don't care about anything else. I want my Alfie to come back. I'm going to move away from here and then that bastard wouldn't know where we are...'

'Don't do anything hasty. Think about it for a bit. How would you provide for yourself and the boys? He left me a sizeable sum but it wouldn't be enough to keep you for more than a year or two. We don't know where he is and if you move away he'll never find you.'

'Give me the letter, Sarah. Let me read it for myself.' There was only the sound of sniffing as she scanned the contents and examined the banknotes. 'He still loves us – he says so. He would come back if he could. We'll just have to pray that Hatch dies because I can't think of any other way that will allow my Alfie to live with us again.'

'Let's not dwell on it. At least you now know my brother hasn't forgotten you, that he would be at your side if he could. He's clever and resourceful and I'm sure he'll find a way eventually. We just have to be patient.'

Betty blew her nose and dried her eyes. 'There's two pounds here – I can buy my boys some Christmas gifts. Let's go downstairs again. The children will wonder where we've gone. By the by, do we have permission to have a party for Mary?'

'It will be a sorry affair compared to the parties we've had in the past for the children. But as long as we have a cake, presents, and a delicious high tea, I'm sure the children will be satisfied.'

John had now joined the children in the parlour. She studied him closely but could see nothing untoward about his appearance or behaviour. He was as cheerful, loving and well behaved as he had always been. Perhaps he was staying out of the house because Spot was no longer welcome anywhere apart from the scullery.

Betty said she would speak to Sally – one of the girls originally employed as a maid-of-all-work, who had proved an excellent cook and been promoted to this role. The girl would need to know their requirements for the family party.

As Sarah sat watching her progeny play she had ample time to consider how things had changed in the past few weeks. She was almost certain her mother had started to have ideas above her station shortly after Hatch had visited.

Obviously, this was a coincidence as that wretched man could have nothing to do with her mother's changed behaviour. The fact that not only Alfie, but also Joe and Robert had gone meant the balance in the house had changed. Ma was the oldest and owned the lease for the property they were living in, so it was hardly surprising she was exerting her authority in this way.

In future Sarah intended to put away an extra pound or two each week; she had a nasty, sinking feeling in the pit of her stomach that sometime in the future she was going to need it.

Mary was overjoyed with the miniature crib Davie had made her for her birthday. Sarah had sewn an entire wardrobe of little garments to fit the new rag doll that Betty had made. Significantly, there was no gift from her daughter's grandmother.

Her oldest son had been given permission to leave his work at three o'clock so that he could attend the special birthday tea. John had helped with the decorations in the parlour and Betty had occupied the children upstairs so the surprise would not be spoiled.

'There, Ma,' John said, 'I reckon it looks perfect. Not just Mary, but Tommy and Jimmy will be that impressed. It ain't like the parties what we had when our pa was alive, but better than nothing.'

'It certainly is, young man. She is a very lucky little girl to be having a party at all. We shall all join in the games and I'm sure Mary will enjoy every moment.'

'I meant no disrespect, Ma, but no one laughs much nowadays. I'll be glad when you marry Uncle Robert and you can move away from here. Mrs Rand don't take kindly to children, if you want my opinion.'

She was too shocked to find her engagement was no secret to comment on the criticism of her mother. 'How long have you known? I wanted to keep it quiet until I was sure he was on his way home.'

'I reckon anyone who saw you together could work it out like I did. I don't know why you've waited so long. Was it because you thought Joe, John and me would be upset to see you marry again?'

'No, I knew you would be happy for me. It was because Betty had just been abandoned by Uncle Alfie and I've no wish to upset her further. Does John know?'

'Course he does, Ma, we've talked it over. I'll stop here in Chelmsford and lodge at the workshop but he'll come with you to Colchester.'

She smiled sadly. 'How quickly you have grown up – first Joe and now you. Your father would have been so proud of you. You have turned into a fine young man.'

'We'll not say nothing to Auntie Betty, but I reckon she'd take it all right now. None of us like it here any more – we're not welcome.'

'Davie, you mustn't say such things. Remember our circumstances before my mother took us in and gave us such a luxurious home? It's all very well to cavil now, but we could have ended up in the workhouse.'

Instead of being shocked by her remark he laughed. 'Come off it, Ma, Uncle Alfie would have taken care of us. In fact, it might have been better if we hadn't moved in with Mrs Rand because then he would have been the man of the house and not buggered off to London.'

'That might well be true, but Hatch and his men would have found him and either your uncle would be awaiting the gallows for murder or Hatch would have had him killed and got away with it.'

A slight sound behind her made her spin round. Her mother was standing there, her face ashen, and she was gripping onto the door frame as if she would collapse in a heap if she let go.

'Ma, I am so sorry that you overheard this conversation…' Sarah wasn't sure how long her mother had been eavesdropping.

'Sarah, how can you say such things about Mr Hatch? He told me he was looking for Alfie because he was the best employee he had ever had. He wants to offer him a permanent position in his business. Wherever did you get the preposterous notion that he had come to harm your brother?'

'I know more about the man than you do after one short meeting, Ma. He's not a businessman, he's a criminal and wants to harm Alfie not help him.'

'I'm shocked to hear you say so, Sarah.' She moved into the room and looked around at the brightly coloured bunting. 'This looks very pretty. I have a gift for my granddaughter but thought I would keep it until this afternoon. Have you seen the cake? I'm sure the children will love it.'

Davie nodded to her and slipped out without comment. There would be time enough to discuss what they knew when they could be sure of not being overheard. She pushed her concerns to one side. 'We're having some games and then will have our tea. That's why the furniture has been temporally rearranged.'

'Blind man's buff? Musical chairs?'

'Yes, and pin the tail on the donkey. As nobody is able to play the piano we shall have to sing for the music.'

'It sounds as if you will have a jolly time. I shall join you for tea, but I have an important customer coming to the shop so cannot be there for the games.'

'I can hear the children coming downstairs, Ma. We had better close the door or they will see the preparations too soon.'

Her mother whisked away, leaving Sarah with much to dwell on. The children were eager to get out into the garden as it had been snowing since first light. There was paperwork to attend to but today it could wait as she intended to devote her entire attention to her daughter.

Three snowmen were built and then a lively game of snowballs took place until they were all cold, wet and exhausted.

'That were grand, Ma. We ain't had so much fun since I can't remember when,' John said as he stamped the snow from his boots before going into the scullery.

'You just have time to change into your Sunday best and then it will be time for the birthday tea.'

She snatched up her daughter who was red-faced and cold, but Sarah had never seen her so happy. 'Come along, sweetheart, we shall get into dry clothes.'

Betty was carrying Jimmy, and Tommy was trailing along behind her whining that he was cold and wet. 'That's quite enough of that nonsense, young man. If you want to come down for the special tea you had better mind your manners,' his mother said briskly.

'I do want to come, I do. Will there be cake and jelly?'

'There certainly will, and I believe there are going to be scones and jam as well as dainty sandwiches and hot sausages.'

This was enough to quell the complaints and the little boy was as happy as his cousin as he dashed into the small bedchamber he shared with Jimmy.

Ma's gift for Sarah's daughter was a new outfit, which was lying ready on the bed when they went in to change.

'You must promise not to mire your new dress, Mary, so no rolling around on the floor. Do you promise me?'

The little girl nodded vigorously. 'I'll keep it spotless, Ma. It's ever so pretty, and Grandma's even made me pantalettes and petticoats.'

Sarah was about to help her daughter put on the new, beautifully embroidered petticoat when Mary stopped her.

'If I wear these I won't be able to play the games. I'll keep it for church and wear the blue one. The one you made me.'

'What a sensible and grown-up girl you are, love. I think you've made a wise choice. Quickly now, let's get dressed so we can go downstairs and the fun can begin.'

The three younger children loved every minute but, however much she tried to enjoy it, she could not help comparing it in her mind to the last party that had been held for Joe, Davie and John the summer before Dan had died. She had missed it because she was taking care of Alfie who had been badly beaten up by Hatch's minions. Recalling this incident made her even more determined to set her mother straight about this man. Hatch was personable enough, looked like a gentleman, but was a villain through and through.

That night she found it difficult to sleep. Hatch had already been notorious in the part of Colchester that they had lived before the tragedy so her mother must be well aware of the man's true character. Why then was she now talking of him so fondly?

Sarah could not help but think they were fortunate indeed to live in such spacious accommodation. Tommy and Jimmy had their own room, she shared with Mary, and Davie and John had another chamber to themselves. Her mother had what could almost be called an apartment to herself as she had a dressing room, a bedroom and a small boudoir.

In all there were six rooms upstairs and as many down, although the two largest had been utilised as the shop and the sewing room. The three girls, one too many in her opinion, shared a comfortable attic room. There were also two further reasonable rooms up there, which were already furnished. Perhaps the previous owners of this property had a dozen children to accommodate.

All they had to do was remain put until Robert came home and then they would all move to an equally luxurious home in Lexden, a fashionable area of Colchester.

8

WHITECHAPEL, DECEMBER 1848

Fred was incensed when he heard what had happened to Alfie. 'Why don't you put in for married quarters? They won't be as grand as what your missus is used to, but at least you'll be together.'

'I ain't bringing them up here. There's cholera rife and congestion of the lungs, not to mention the danger from the folk living in this rough area. No, I ain't doing that. She knows I care for her – that'll have to do for the moment.' He wasn't sure if he should share his half-formed notion with his friend or keep it to himself.

'Spit it out. There's something you're not telling me.'

Alfie told him about the arrest he had made, and about the interest Inspector Burgess now had in him. 'I want to get into plain-clothes, the Criminal Investigation Division, be a detective. I ain't too keen on wandering about the place in this lot.'

'People don't like them detectives. They think it ain't right to poke about in folks' business, trick folk into doing summat when they don't know it's the police doing it. The peelers ain't liked too much, but them others are thought of even worse.'

'From what I gleaned I ain't got much chance of being picked. There's only a dozen or so and they work at Scotland Yard. Sergeant told me Burgess is hoping to join them.'

'Well, I says good luck to you. Not sure how being in plain-clothes will bring your family together...'

'It's more salubrious round Scotland Yard. Stands to reason, don't it, that married quarters will be better and healthier for Betty and the nippers.'

A week later, on Sunday, he was sent for by the inspector. 'I need you at the Charing Cross Hotel in half an hour. Out of your uniform. Nothing smart mind – I want you looking in a bad state.'

'Yes, sir, I'll be there. Thank you for thinking of me.'

He raced back to his lodgings and found the most disreputable of his civilian clothes and put them on. He rubbed grime on his face and hands, ran his fingers through his hair so it stood up, and made his way speedily to the hotel. His disguise was so excellent the doorman refused him entry.

'Get away with you, you villain; this place is not for the likes of you.'

'Begging your pardon, sir, I was told to report to a gentleman in your bar.'

'I'll make enquiries. You stop where you are or I'll have the law on you.'

Being in disguise, so to speak, Alfie didn't put him straight but had an inward chuckle. Minutes later the doorman returned, apologetic, and escorted him to meet the inspector.

'Good show, Nightingale, you've done well. Set yourself down and hear what the manager of this establishment has to tell us.'

'There's been a number of petty thefts lately from the bedchambers. I suspect the fellow orchestrating these events is walking out with one of my chambermaids. He's been seen in the courtyard beneath the windows at the same time the girl is working in the rooms above.'

Alfie waited to hear what they wanted him to do. Inspector Burgess enlightened him. 'You are to follow this villain and find out all you can about him without revealing yourself.'

That was all he was told to do; the rest was left to him. Alfie couldn't see why, if they knew who the two culprits was, they couldn't apprehend them without going to these lengths. He weren't going to argue though; he were happy to oblige and determined to catch the bugger and add him to his list of arrests.

The inspector had assured him he was cleared for this duty and excused his patrolling until this job were done. Alfie lurked outside the yard until the suspect came out and then followed him to his lodgings. He found himself a battered carpetbag and then went into the shop nearby and enquired as to where he could get lodgings.

'There's a woman two doors down takes in lodgers. I'll speak to her for you.'

'I'd be obliged. I'll leave my bag here – I'm going out to look for work.'

He left it an hour and then returned. 'Mr Smith, I've good news for you. If you're prepared to share a bedroom then you're in luck.'

'That'll do me. I ain't got much rhino spare. Sharing will make it cheaper.'

The room was clean, the bed vermin-free, and the fellow he were investigating was happy enough to have him there. This was a puzzle to Alfie – if he were a criminal the last thing he'd want were a stranger sharing his chamber.

He was about to have a poke about when footsteps on the boards outside warned him he were about to have company. The cove what came in gave him a pleasant smile. 'Bob Smalley, pleased to meet yer.'

'Bert Smith, likewise. You're a gent for letting me share.'

'No trouble. Have yer found work yet?'

'Few days with a carter. Ain't much, but it's a start.'

Alfie didn't want to spend too much time with this thief in case he gave himself away. 'I'm off to find meself some supper.' He didn't give Smalley time to respond but left the room, and then the house, in double quick time.

He was on the way to his usual pie shop but then recalled he was in disguise, so to speak. He'd better find himself somewhere else until this assignment were over. According to the manager of the Charing Cross Hotel, the suspect would be working the next day. If the manager and the inspector knew the cove were receiving stolen goods, then why hadn't he already been arrested?

Not for him to question his betters, but this all seemed an expensive waste of time. He reckoned the chambermaid was tossing out the items through the window and Smalley was catching them in the yard below.

The only reason he could think of for catching the thief in such a laborious way was that the manager didn't want any fuss at his smart hotel.

Next morning he got up early and left as though he was going to work, leaving the other bed occupied. Alfie returned to his temporary lodgings mid-afternoon. He removed his boots, and holding them in one hand, he crept up the stairs and put his ear to the bedroom door.

Smalley was definitely in there and from the sound of it so was his lady-love. The door opened outwards. If he shoved something heavy against it the two of them would be imprisoned inside whilst he returned to his lodgings and put his uniform back on. From what he could hear the two of them were busy in bed so he wouldn't risk making a racket moving furniture but pray they'd still be where he'd left them when he got back.

He called in at the station to find another constable to come with him as he didn't think he could bring two of them back on his own. He explained to the custody sergeant and immediately Constable Riley was sent for. It were a brisk walk down Whitechapel and along Fenchurch Street. There were more taxis around in this part of town and it were too far to walk.

'It's no more than a stone's throw to Scotland Yard from Charing Cross. We can march the pair of them there easy enough,' he told his companion.

'You're a lucky bugger getting friendly like with the inspector. He's taken a shine to you, and no mistake. I've been in the force for more than a year and he's not taken no notice of me.'

'Just luck, mate, that's all. You'll have your name on the docket as an arresting officer. Should help your promotion hopes.'

'I ain't bothered about promotion, but I'm after married quarters so me and my young lady can tie the knot.'

It took a fair while to reach their destination and Alfie carefully noted in his pocketbook how much he'd had to pay the jarvey. He would be reimbursed his expenses – at least he bloody well hoped so, as he was already out of pocket having paid his landlady upfront for the week and the tanner he'd had to pay for the carpetbag.

Smalley and his accomplice were still inside the room. Alfie nodded to Riley and threw back the door. The sudden appearance of two uniformed constables rendered the couple sprawling on the bed speechless.

They were duly arrested and their ill-gotten gains recovered from under the bed. The two were dead to rights, caught red-handed, and they didn't resist arrest. He and Riley turned their backs whilst the bird dragged on some clothes. She seemed pathetically grateful she wasn't to be marched through the streets in a petticoat.

There were numerous forms to fill in. Riley found writing a struggle so Alfie completed the paperwork for him. When he'd done he spoke to the sergeant on the desk.

'Is there something I need to do to claim back me expenses?'

'There is, lad, but it won't come from here, but Leman Street.'

Once outside Scotland Yard he was at a loss as to what he should do next. 'I ain't sure if I'm on nights or days. Bugger me if I know what I'm supposed to be doing now.'

They had decided not to take a cab back as there was no urgency – he were quite enjoying marching through the streets in his uniform with a companion at his side. It took them more than an hour and it were full dark by the time they reported at his home station.

'Inspector Burgess wants to see you before you start your shift tomorrow morning, Nightingale. You've got the remainder of today to yourself.' The sergeant patted the completed expenses sheet. 'I'll see you get this from petty cash when you report in tomorrow.'

The unfortunate Constable Riley weren't so lucky and had to go back to his duties overseeing the prisoners and the cells. It were perishing cold, snowing heavily. Alfie were grateful for the warmth of his thick greatcoat. Today was his niece's birthday – whatever the risks he were determined to see his wife and sons when the weather was better. He couldn't go to Chelmsford, so he would send them a letter and arrange for them to meet him in London.

* * *

Chelmsford, February 1849

Christmas had been somewhat subdued by the absence of Robert, Alfie and Joe. The little ones were scarcely aware of the tension in the house and took great pleasure in their gifts and the abundance of food available. Mary finally wore her new gown to church on Christmas Day and it was much admired.

Sarah could hardly credit how quickly the weeks had flown by since then and still no letters from Robert or Joe. She decided she would take Mary and John to Colchester and visit Ada, who must be equally worried about the lack of correspondence from her favourite adult son.

'Betty, I'm going to Colchester now the weather has improved – I hope you and your boys will accompany me.'

'Ta, I'd love to. A day out would do us all good. I know you've not said anything but you must be concerned about Robert and Joe. I was wondering if there's an authority you could contact for information – perhaps the shipping company might know if they are on their way back to England or still somewhere far away.'

'I thought to ask Ada when we see her. She'll know whether there's anything to be worried about. The weather is clement for the middle of February so shall we go tomorrow? Ma can manage without me and I shall ask Davie to take a note to school excusing John for the day.'

'Will you tell Mrs Rand tonight?'

'She's always more receptive after supper when she has consumed a sweet sherry or two. I am still puzzled by her continued friendship with this Mrs Forsyth especially as you've yet to find anything about the woman.'

'My friend had never heard of her and she knows everyone of importance in Chelmsford. I'm beginning to suspect your mother might be meeting a gentleman friend but doesn't like to tell us.'

Sarah felt her colour draining and clutched the edge of the table to keep herself upright. How could she have been so blind? She felt her breakfast threatening to return and swallowed hastily.

'I know exactly who she's seeing. It's Hatch. It explains her furtive behaviour and the way she jumped to his defence when I spoke of him a few months ago. I cannot believe she's so gullible. If she marries him he will own everything, have control over our lives. He will have his perfect revenge on Alfie.'

The conversation was interrupted as Jimmy howled when he fell and banged his head on the floor and by the time Betty had soothed him she had recovered her equilibrium.

'Surely she would not be so foolish as to marry him? Give up everything she's got just for a bit of how's your father?'

'If she imagines herself in love then she will do anything. That man will convince her he's a pillar of society, and an honest businessman, that he will be delighted to take us all under his wing and care for us as if we were his own flesh and blood.'

'She couldn't be so stupid, not after everything we've told her about him.'

'I wish I could believe that. The more I think about it, Betty, the more convinced I am that our lives are about to be turned upside down. I thank the Lord that I've been putting money away against that day. We don't have a fortune, but we have more than most folk see in one place in a lifetime. It should be sufficient to rent a decent house and set up another workshop.'

'We can't do that here. There's no room for two businesses making clothes for ladies and children in Chelmsford. Where shall we go?'

'If Hatch is moving here then it will be safe for us return to Colchester. I'm not going to rush headlong into anything. We have to be sure of our facts before we leave.'

'Those men who were watching the house and the station have gone, so Hatch can't be expecting Alfie to come back. We must ask Davie's friend at the station to check if Mrs Rand takes the train to Colchester or if Hatch comes here on the days that she goes out. I think we should be able to confirm or deny our fears in a week or so.'

'Ada might well know something. If she doesn't then she can get one of her numerous children to make enquiries in Stockwell Street whilst we're there. Whatever happens, Betty, we will stay together.'

'I was hoping Alfie would send me a letter. Now we have the penny post there's no risk of anyone getting hold of it and reading the contents.'

'Do you get to the mail before my mother every morning and afternoon?'

Betty shook her head. 'She wouldn't take it, would she? Do you think he's written and your mother's stolen the letter?'

'Perhaps I'm being overdramatic, but I honestly think if she's been duped by that man, thinks she's in love with him and he with her, she would do anything he asked. I pray that I'm wrong, but I have a nasty suspicion that I'm not.'

After consideration she and Betty decided not to tell her mother they were going to Colchester the next day in case she sent word to Hatch. Davie was only too happy to ask his friend to keep an eye out at the station.

'I reckon you could be right, Ma. Mrs Rand is always dressed in her best gown when she goes out for the day. Ladies like to look their best for their gentlemen friends.'

'What do you know about it, young man? I hope you're not going to start courting until your apprenticeship is done. Can you arrange to lodge there at such short notice if we moved?'

'He'd be delighted to have me – means he can get me to work longer hours if I'm on the premises. I get an afternoon off every week and can come to Colchester to see you all.'

The children didn't know they were going on the train. Telling them would mean that the entire household would know within an hour or so. The next morning she and Betty behaved as usual. She had already written a note for Davie to drop into the school and he'd left with it before they came down.

'Ma, why do I have to put on my Sunday best today?' Mary asked. 'And why have you got on yours as well?'

'It's a secret. You'll find out after breakfast.'

She had arranged for a simple meal of toast and tea to be served at seven o'clock. Her mother never appeared until eight o'clock, and they would be on the train by then. John had got up with his brother and taken the dog for a long walk so he wouldn't object to being shut in the garden all day. He had wanted to bring Spot with him, but she had refused.

Betty was smiling and she found herself returning it. 'It's a lovely day, Sarah, perfect for an outing.' This was said quietly so the children didn't hear. Only as they left the house by the side gate at seven thirty did she reveal the surprise.

'We are going to Colchester to visit Uncle Robert's siblings and his mother. We are going to travel on the train.'

Mary and Tommy had arrived by train but had been too small to remember it now. The announcement was greeted with squeals of excitement. Hearing her daughter and nephew so joyful lifted her spirits and helped her to push aside her worries about the future.

By happenstance they passed the postman with his bulging bag about to start his round. 'Excuse me, Mrs Nightingale and I have been expecting letters but we are concerned they could have been mislaid. Mine would be somewhat dirty as they would be coming from India; Mrs Nightingale's would be coming from London.'

The man scratched his head, knocking his smart peaked cap to one side. 'That's right strange, missus, as I delivered one for Mrs Nightingale a few weeks back. Not had anything for you personal like, sorry.'

'Thank you, it must be somewhere in the house,' Betty said with false gaiety.

John had run ahead holding the hands of the children whilst Betty carried Jimmy in a sling made from a shawl.

'I knew it – your mother has intercepted my letter. She must have been told to look out for a London postmark. I don't get mail from anyone so it must have been easy for her to do it.'

'I fear that you're right. It merely confirms what we suspect. I wish the postman had said there had been letters for me. I wouldn't care if they'd been stolen by my mother; at least I would know Robert and Joe are well.'

The hour-long journey to Colchester was accomplished without mishap. Only as they were disembarking did it occur to her she should have let Ada know they were coming.

'I hope she's at home, otherwise it will be a wasted journey.'

'Where else would she be?' Betty replied.

'Remember, all her children will be at school now for the morning so she could well go out.'

'With so many to take care of I expect she's sitting in the kitchen with her feet up enjoying some peace and quiet. On the other hand, maybe she's doing the ironing or cleaning the house or…'

'Enough, Betty, you've made your point. Robert told me Ada now has a maid to help her as well as a woman coming in every day to do the heavy work. He's a good man, and I expect you've already guessed we have an understanding.'

Instead of being offended that this information had been kept from her, her friend laughed. 'Even a blind man could see he was besotted with you and just waiting for you to realise you returned his feelings. I pray every night that he and Joe come back safely – you lost enough already when Dan died.'

John, who had been playing with the children overheard the remark. 'Pa would be pleased, Ma. He'd want you to be happy. I was reading that gent's newspaper over his shoulder whilst we was waiting for the train – said that hundreds of folks are dying from the cholera in London. You don't want to be moving there, even to be with Uncle Alfie, Auntie Betty.'

9

WHITECHAPEL, FEBRUARY 1849

Alfie hadn't put the address of his lodgings in the letter as he didn't wish Betty or Sarah to know that he'd become a member of the Metropolitan Police. Instead he'd sent another ten-bob note to cover the cost of the train fares – more than enough – but he wanted her to have a bit extra to buy herself something nice. He asked her to travel on the morning train from Chelmsford on the day that he would be changing from nights to days. This meant he had ample time to return home and change into his civilian clothes before going to meet her.

In the weeks since his plain-clothes job for the inspector he'd had a quiet time of it. He'd made more than a dozen arrests, but none of them were for more than misdemeanours, petty pilfering and such. Every time he checked in at the Leman Road police station he hoped to see Burgess but from what he could learn the inspector had now transferred permanently to Scotland Yard.

His hopes of becoming a detective faded and he resigned himself to seeking promotion from a constable to a sergeant, but he would have to put in a year or two before that happened. Eventually the day arrived when his family would be coming to see him. Fortunately, today he had no miscreants to march to the magistrates so was able to leave at the end of his shift. He took particular trouble over his appearance, put on his best garments and headed for the station in high spirits.

He waited on the platform and watched the train steam in. His heart was thudding, his palms clammy; he'd never been so nervous. His boys would have changed so much since he'd last seen them. Six months was a long time and he expected Jimmy to have forgotten who he was, but he thought that Tommy would still remember him.

The doors were thrown back and the passengers began to descend. The clouds of steam made it almost impossible to see along the platform. He watched and waited until everyone had departed. They hadn't come. Betty had made it quite clear she no longer wished to have any contact with him. That part of his life were over. It would be better for her if he were dead and she could find herself a decent husband, one what didn't run off because his pride were hurt.

He swallowed the lump in his throat and angrily brushed his eyes with his sleeve. From now on would be a better man, put money aside and one day, when he had made something of himself, he would go back and give it to them. Until then he must rely on his sister to take care of his family in his absence.

His appetite had deserted him and he didn't drop into his usual haunt for a meat pie and a mug of tea. He would regret this later, but the last thing on his mind was filling his belly. The cottage were empty. Fred and the other two would be eating breakfast so he had the place to himself. He buffed up his boots, checked that his uniform buttons were shiny, his top hat brushed smooth, and was then ready to go to Scotland Yard and fill in an application to become a detective.

There was only a few in this division. His chances of getting a place was slim, but unless he put his name down, them that were in charge wouldn't know he was interested. The desk sergeant recognised him.

'Constable Nightingale, what can I do for you today?'

Alfie explained why he'd come and instead of laughing at his presumption the sergeant pursed his lips and nodded. 'You would be ideally suited for this new division, lad. I'll make sure Inspector Burgess sees your application. As far as I know they aren't expanding their numbers at present, but if you continue to make a good impression at Leman Street there's a good chance you will get in eventually.'

'Thank you, sir, that's exactly what I wanted to hear.' He took the form and in his best copperplate completed it. He checked it through twice more and then handed it in.

The sergeant perused it. 'Good, good, a neat hand and no spelling mistakes. This will make a good impression.'

The wages for a detective wasn't a lot more than he were getting now, but despite the fact that Betty had chosen not to visit, he hadn't abandoned all hope that one day they would be a family again. When they was he would need to have decent married quarters, not bring them to the squalid streets where he were living now.

Two constables on a different beat had lost family members to cholera recently. It didn't bear thinking about. To lose a child must be the hardest thing to deal with. No, he was now glad they hadn't come and risked possible infection by being in the city. He would write again in a week or two, say that he understood, but he loved them and hoped they could all be together one day.

In a better frame of mind he decided to spend a tanner on a taxi and travel back in style. He grabbed a pie and coffee but knew better than to eat them in view of the public. Once in the cottage he devoured his meal and then joined his fellow constables for a few hours' shut-eye before starting the next four weeks of night duties.

* * *

Colchester, February 1849

'If we cut through by the river and then go alongside the castle it will be quicker and more interesting for the children. John, do you remember Colchester at all?'

'Course I do, Ma, I ain't a baby. I was six when we left, old enough to remember lots.'

'Good, then you can go ahead with Mary and Tommy. Wait for us when you get to the bridge. I don't want you going near the river unless Auntie Betty and I are there.'

The road was busy with carts, carriages and diligences and it took them some time to cross safely. Once they were on the correct side of the road she gave John permission to go.

'It's strange being back here after more than two years, isn't it, Sarah? It seems busier, but still more like home than Chelmsford does.'

'This is a more prosperous town despite the fact that Chelmsford is supposed to be the centre of Essex. It used to be a military town but when the war against Napoleon ended they closed the barracks.'

'From what I heard from my grandma the area around Magdalen Street was mostly brothels – if you want my opinion it was a good thing the soldiers left.'

This was an odd conversation to be having as neither of them were particularly interested in history and certainly not in brothels or soldiers. Perhaps they were both trying to avoid talking about their worries for the future.

'Let me carry little Jimmy for a bit. You must be exhausted.'

'I was sitting down on the train. I'm not at all tired.'

They turned into the lane that would lead to the water meadows and John was waiting for them. They crossed the bridge together and then once they were a safe distance from the water she allowed them to run ahead.

'I can't wait to move back here. I've been thinking, Betty, about where to look for a rented property for us all. I would like somewhere with a garden for the children to play in but it has to be in an area that our customers will walk past.'

'What about Trinity Street? We could walk back that way and see if anything's available.'

Sarah was silent for a minute and then mentioned a subject she had been avoiding. 'Do you believe that Robert and Joe have been lost at sea?'

'You haven't heard anything for six months. They were supposed to be on their way home by now. The way things are with Mrs Rand and Hatch I reckon it would be sensible to be ready to leave if needs be. Now I know that my Alfie wrote to me, I'm not so bothered that he's away. I'm certain he'll come back when he's good and ready.'

'I know he will. I just wish I knew whether *The Empress* and its crew are safe somewhere. Robert's ship didn't leave from Harwich, it left from London. If it wasn't for the cholera epidemic I'd go there and make enquiries myself.'

She gathered the children together and they crossed East Hill and began the walk down St Botolph's Street. Fortunately, this was downhill, which made walking easier.

'Ma, Ma, will you carry me? My legs hurt ever so much,' Mary whinged when they were halfway there.

'I certainly will not, young lady, you are a big girl now and can walk on your own. It's not far now. Mrs Billings lives close to the big church. Can you see the tower behind those houses?'

They could and the thought that they only had a short distance to walk stopped the complaints. When they turned into the small street she pointed out the house to John.

'Run ahead and knock on door. Mrs Billings doesn't know we are about to descend on her.' She exchanged an anxious glance with Betty. She had no idea what they would do if her friend wasn't at home.

Her worries proved unfounded as Ada opened the door and dashed into the street in her house slippers to greet them. 'My, what a lovely surprise. It must be almost a year since I saw you last. Come in, come in, I can't tell you how pleased I am to see you.'

'And I you. I was saying to Betty that all your children will be at school. Is that the case?'

'Good heavens, no, three are still at school but the oldest three are all in employment. I'm not standing out here talking to you a moment longer. I have just baked and there's vegetable soup simmering on the range. Plenty for everyone.'

She led the way into the house and it held little resemblance to the place Sarah had found refuge in all those years ago. Now it was freshly painted, everything spick and span and they were led into the front parlour and not the kitchen.

'I have Molly to help me now as well as the laundry and scrubbing done. Apart from a bit of mending, I'm a lady of leisure. My Robert takes care of us.' Her smile slipped. 'I know why you've come. He told me you were intending to get married when he returned. I've heard nothing for months – I take it you've heard nothing either?'

'No, I was hoping you might know to whom I could make enquiries. I know these long sea voyages can take months more than expected but I did think I might have had another letter by now.'

'I've got the details somewhere. But I warn you, Sarah love, it's unlikely anyone will know. Unless news has come from another ship, the owners will be as much in the dark as we are. They have a board in every customs office in all the ports and they write which ships have come in and which are still at sea.'

'Has this happened before?'

'It has once or twice, so I'm not too worried at the moment. *The Empress* is due to dock in London in June – if we hear nothing by September then I think... I think they might have perished.'

This conversation had been held in the spacious entrance hall. John had already taken Mary and Tommy into the parlour to investigate the toy box.

Jimmy struggled to be put down. He was desperate to join the others. His wails of protest interrupted the conversation.

'No, baby, I need to change your bottom first,' Betty said firmly. 'Is there somewhere I can go to do this?'

'You go ahead and do it in here, love. I've changed enough backsides in here in my time.'

The children were content and playing happily under the window. Jimmy, clean and fresh again, was tottering about babbling to himself and Ada was arranging for luncheon to be served in the dining room.

Sarah turned to Betty. 'I shall try not to imagine the worst until June. If Ada isn't concerned, and she's got several sons and a husband at sea, then I shall not be either.'

Ada returned after speaking to her maid. 'I have some gossip for you, Sarah, and I think it might well interest you too, Betty.' She took a seat next to the fire and had their full attention. 'Mr Hatch has been going regularly to Chelmsford and word is that he has a lady friend there. My boy Billy is working for the man who bought Alfie's house and business. He hears a lot of things – no one takes any notice of a delivery boy.' She hadn't finished with her revelations. 'He's also heard that Hatch's empire is crumbling. We've got a larger police force here and most of his employees are now in custody. He's got to move if he doesn't want to end up inside himself.'

'I knew it. We suspected that my mother was involved with him; now you've confirmed our worst fears. When she marries him, he will have power over us and I'm not going to let that happen. It also explains why he's so eager to get his hands on her business.' Sarah explained one of the reasons they'd come and immediately Ada offered to look after the children so that she and Betty could investigate premises.

'You can't move back until he's gone, but it will be grand having you in Colchester again. When Robert returns he'll come here when he can't find you in Chelmsford.'

Sarah looked at the handsome overmantel clock. 'We're catching the three o'clock train and it takes an hour to walk to North Station so we must leave here by two. It's ten thirty now, which means we have an hour and a half before you serve lunch.'

'Then you'd better get going, love. It isn't far if you're thinking of Trinity Street – it's this side of town. What with Mr Hyam's factory just up the road from here, it'll be an ideal place to set up your ready-made garment business. Seamstresses are in short supply here as most of the work is done at home by the women.'

'I'd thought of that. Four of the girls employed in Chelmsford are loyal to me, not my mother, and I'm hoping I might persuade them to accompany us if I can offer them decent accommodation.'

The sun shone and she took this as a sign that she'd made the right decision. They cut through Short Wyre Street, a narrow, congested lane with overcrowded cottages and an air of neglect about it.

'This is a depressing place. Surely, being so close to somewhere that offers regular employment it should be in a better state?'

Betty was holding her handkerchief over her nose and mouth, trying not to gag at the appalling smell coming from the filthy gutters and didn't answer. These cottages backed onto the Roman wall that still partially encircled Colchester and there would be no room for the night soil collector to empty the privies. The smell brought back unpleasant memories of her short time living in an even poorer environment in the worst part of town. Dan had rescued her from this degradation.

They hastened along Eld Lane, which was not as noxious as Short Wyre Street, holding their skirts out of the mire as best they could, and were grateful to reach Trinity Street. This thoroughfare was altogether different, the cobbles swept clean, the pavements safe to walk on and the buildings on either side were better cared for.

'Thank the good Lord for that. I don't remember it being so unpleasant in this area. If this is a prosperous town why haven't they done something about the lack of plumbing here?' Betty shook out her skirts and looked around with appreciation. 'There are dwelling houses, and a few small shops on the right side of the road. On this side some of the buildings are bigger. I don't think we'll be able to afford anything suitable there.'

'There's a small milliner's just ahead, and next to it a haberdasher's shop. I think this would be a perfect place to open my business if we can find something that will work. We need accommodation for the seamstresses, a maid plus chambers for ourselves.'

'There must also be somewhere to convert into the workroom and a decent frontage onto the street so passing ladies can see examples of our gowns and children's wear,' Betty replied.

The road was too narrow to allow carriages to pass safely but this didn't prevent the owners of such vehicles from attempting to do so. They were obliged to leap to safety into a carriage archway to avoid being trampled. They remained where they were, watching the drivers attempting to achieve the almost impossible.

Sarah, becoming bored with the spectacle, turned round and saw the archway led into a pretty courtyard and garden. The house it belonged to was of ancient construction, timbered with overhanging eaves and leaded windows. There was a large carriage house and stables at the rear of the garden.

'Betty, this place is unoccupied.'

'It might well be, but it's too grand for the likes of us. This is the house of a gentleman. We could never afford to rent it even if we knew who owned it.'

'That might very well be true, but shall we look anyway? I think it's in reasonable repair but has been empty for some time.'

They pressed their noses against each window in turn but they could see little of the dark interior through the filthy panes. When the racket in the street ceased they continued on their walk but found nothing that appealed to Sarah as much as the empty house.

'We have plenty of time. Where shall we look next? I fear nothing will come up to my high expectations after seeing the house in Trinity Street.'

Betty nudged her. 'Maybe when Robert comes back you can rent it. He'll be a captain then and able to afford to keep you in luxury.'

'I shall bear it in mind. Now, what about having a look North Hill? I know it's close to Hatch's domain, but we'll only be moving here if he moves to Chelmsford.'

They walked slowly past the church and were about halfway down the hill when they saw an empty shop. Details of who to apply to were written on a notice pinned in the window. Sarah's heart thumped. Her mouth was dry. She pointed to the words in faded gold above the door.

'Nightingale, R, Clothier, Bespoke Outfitter and Hosier.'

This was fate. No relative of hers had owned this place but having the same name meant this was where she was meant to be. She had found her next home.

10

CHELMSFORD, MARCH 1849

Sarah was no longer able to put money openly into her account as her mother now insisted on paying in the weekly takings herself. After a deal of soul-searching she decided to take her wages out of the cash before she entered anything into the books. This way felt dishonest, but she needed to protect the interests of her family.

The weather continued to improve and the garden was full of daffodils and primroses. Betty made sure she caught the postman before he delivered the letters and one morning she rushed in to the office, her face radiant.

'Sarah, Alfie's written again.' She tore open the envelope and her expression changed to horror. 'We were to go and see him in London last month but when we didn't turn up he thought I wanted no more of him. He doesn't put his address – how can I tell him I didn't get his first letter?'

'You can't. He says he will contact you again in the future in the hope that you might have changed your mind. You must hang on to that. There's nothing else you can do at the moment. I'm glad you came in as there's something we need to discuss.'

Betty checked the passageway was clear and then pulled the door shut. 'Have you heard from the solicitors in Colchester about that property on North Hill?'

'I have. Unfortunately it is a repairing lease, which means we will be responsible for keeping the fabric of the building in good order. I can't agree until I've seen inside – it could well be falling down for all we know.' She perused the letter again. 'It would seem I can call in at any time to collect the keys. However, there are other interested parties and they need a decision in the next few days.'

'Go today. If you hurry you'll catch the mid-morning train. How long do you think it will take to view this property?'

'Not long. If it's satisfactory I'll sign the papers before I come home. I should like to bring our furniture with us but I fear we'll have to sneak away like debtors...'

'Between us we can carry all our garments – we'll just have to purchase the other things we need.' She clapped a hand to her mouth and squealed as if stuck by a hatpin. 'The man Alfie sold his business to still has my furniture and such – he always promised to bring it to us. Do you think he might still let me have it, even after so long?'

'I'll call in and speak to him. East Stockwell Street is no distance from North Hill so there will be ample time. I'll write a note just in case he's out when I call.'

Betty had left one of the girls in charge of the children, not something Ma approved of, so her friend hurried off to resume her duties. Sarah kept her personal bank book on her person at all times, so her mother had no idea how much money she had put by.

Davie had confirmed that her ma was meeting Hatch at the Saracens every week so it was only a matter of time before the announcement of a marriage would be made. This meant she had to move quickly if she was to secure the future – she never wished to be in the position she had been when dismissed from her job as under nurse at Grey Friars House and had sunk into destitution.

Then she had been little more than a girl; now she was an independent woman and determined to provide for her children, Betty and the boys, and herself. She pushed away the intrusive thought that Robert might be lost to her. She refused to think about the lack of news from either him or Joe – if she was to be a captain's wife then she would have to learn to live her life without fear. Being constantly worried that your beloved husband could drown wasn't a sensible way to live one's life.

She slipped upstairs and put on her best bonnet, added the new cape she had just finished sewing, found her reticule and gloves, and was ready to depart. If she didn't leave immediately she would have to run to catch the train and she had no intention of doing something so undignified.

The brisk walk from the station at Colchester to the solicitor's office in Head Street was invigorating. She collected the keys to number sixty and told the clerk behind the desk that if the property was suitable she would sign the lease when she returned.

'I shall inform Mr Copping and he will have documents ready, Mrs Cooper.' He peered over his spectacles. 'Which bank do you intend to utilise for your business, madam?'

'I thought to transfer my account to the bank that Mr Bawtree of Grey Friars House is a partner of. I shall call in before I return to Chelmsford and get this organised – that is, if I do find the property satisfactory for my needs.'

The elderly, black-garbed gentleman smiled and noted something on his pad. 'Excellent, I shall inform Mr Copping that you have everything in place.'

The keys were too large to fit in her cloth bag so she was obliged to hold them beneath her cape as she dashed back down the hill to examine what she hoped would become her new home and the start of her own ready-made garment business. Mr Hyam and his sons had yet to venture into making clothes for women and children, which was fortunate for her, as she could not possibly compete with his prices.

She walked under the archway to the rear of the property. She pulled out the keys and decided the largest one was most likely to fit the wrought-iron gate. She was correct in her assumption and stepped into a paved area, the flagstones green with moss and slippery to walk on. The windows here were obscured with sacks so she couldn't look in.

She walked to the end of the recently constructed extension to the older building and through a second gate, this time of wood and unlocked, and discovered an overgrown, weed-infested garden. It might not look much now, but with a little attention it would be exactly what she wanted. There appeared to be no pump or privy outside – could this mean there was indoor plumbing?

The rear door opened smoothly – this was a good sign. If the wood hadn't warped after the property had been left empty for so long it was likely there was no damp.

There was the scuttle of rodents, but that was only to be expected. Their cat would soon deal with this problem. Although it was midday she could see nothing with the windows covered. Leaving the back door open she pulled down the sacking. Welcome light flooded into the room.

This wasn't the kitchen, or indeed the scullery; this had been the office if the abandoned table and chair were any indication. She walked from this space into a long, gaslit workshop. She could scarcely contain her excitement. There were already benches for her girls to sit at, a long, central table for pattern and material cutting. There were even half a dozen moth-eaten cloth dummies – these would be perfectly serviceable once cleaned and repaired.

Mr Nightingale had obviously not sold his business; perhaps the poor man had died and the owners of the property had been unable to find another outfitter to take it over. There were two further doors to explore in the office area. She pushed the first open and discovered there was indeed a water closet. Small wonder the poor man had gone out of business – such things were a luxury few small businesses could afford.

There was a steep wooden staircase to the upper level. Here again she heard the distinctive patter of rats and mice. These chambers had been used as storerooms but would be ideal for accommodation for the girls she hoped to entice away from Chelmsford when she left.

She stepped through into the old part of the house. Here there were low ceilings, soot-blackened beams and an all-pervasive smell of disuse and damp. The kitchen to her left was dismal, but nothing compared to the one in the derelict cottage she and the children had lived in when she had taken the family to live with her unpleasant grandparents. On the positive side there was a sink in the scullery with running water and a small laundry room with a copper that was also plumbed in.

Half of the front of the building was given over to the shop. There were shelves, a long wooden counter, but little else to recommend it. The family quarters had a dining room and one further reception room that looked out onto the pavement of North Hill.

The wooden staircase creaked ominously as she climbed. As half the downstairs area was given over to the shop, upstairs there were six bedrooms. Three of excellent size and three smaller, but more than adequate for her purposes. The attics under the eaves had been occupied by birds and bats as well as rodents. She thought it unlikely she would disturb the present occupants. Whilst there she looked at the roof and could see no obvious problems.

These premises were too good to be true. Once the repairs and renovations had been completed it would be a perfect home for them all. If Robert, no, when Robert came home in the summer and they got married, Betty could continue to live here in comfort and hopefully her brother would return and live there too.

Delighted with her visit she returned to the solicitor's office and signed both copies of the lease without a second thought. She blotted her signature, carefully folded her copy and put it in her bag to be studied in depth at a later date.

'I shall expect the payment to be transferred by the end of the month,' Mr Copping told her.

Sarah had paid a ten-pound deposit, a third of the amount owed, and she thought this more than sufficient. 'As I showed you my bank book you are aware I'm a woman of means. I shall get my account transferred as soon as I can, but as you know these things can take time.'

For the first time his benevolent smile vanished to be replaced by a frown. 'As I informed you, Mrs Cooper, there are others interested in this prime property. The owners wish to have the matter settled by the end of the month as they are leaving the country and will be uncontactable for a year or more.'

'I have signed the lease and it has been witnessed. I am now the leaseholder; the matter is settled.' She rose and slowly put on her gloves. The atmosphere was arctic. Too bad – next time she would deal with the other partner. Mr Copping wasn't someone she wished to do business with again.

* * *

Whitechapel, March 1849

Alfie preferred night duty, when the only interruption to his beat would be from a miscreant, whereas during the day a constable might be stopped numerous times to sort out petty disputes. He was on the lookout for a canary, usually a young woman, an accomplice of a burglary gang, who was given the task of carrying the tools of the trade. She was called a canary as she was required to sing out if there was danger and thus warn her accomplices.

This meant that the actual burglars could stroll about the place looking like gents in their fine clothes and, if apprehended, there would be nothing to charge them with. He'd heard that a constable on another beat had been fooled by one of these girls who had pretended to be having a fit. He had been obliged to take her to the nearest hospital. This meant the burglars had half an hour in which to enter the premises and escape with their loot.

Several nights went by with nothing more exciting than the apprehension of a couple of drunks. It was well known that burglars often used the premises of a public house in order to access the rear of the building what they intended to burgle. Therefore, it were customary for one or other of the constables on this particular beat to investigate the local public houses at least twice every night.

As he was approaching one of these places he noticed a familiar face slip inside. This was a regular offender and someone he recognised immediately. He followed the man and went up to the landlady.

'That fellow and his companion, they are burglars. Did they have anyone else with them?'

'They did indeed, constable, but I'm buggered if I know where the bleeder's gone.'

'Do I have your permission to search the house? I reckon he's inside helping himself to your valuables.'

Alfie edged his way through the door, hoping his arrival would go unnoticed. He pressed himself against the wall and listened. Yes – there was definitely someone creeping about upstairs. He pulled out his stick and gripped it firmly in his good hand before beginning to climb the staircase.

The intruder must have heard him because he no longer attempted to conceal his presence but thundered up the stairs towards the attics with Alfie in hot pursuit.

'There's nowhere to go. You're under arrest for breaking and entering.' He was speaking to an empty room. Had he made an error? Surely the burglar couldn't have got past him? Then he saw footprints on the carpet and realised the man had scrambled out of the window and onto the roof.

He pulled himself through the window and saw the man he was hoping to apprehend hastily removing his boots before throwing the cash box he had stolen to his waiting accomplice, and then vanishing over the side of the building and down a water spout into a stable yard.

Alfie sprung his rattle and swung it around his head. Fred appeared at a run in the street below and took off after the villain. There was nothing more he could do so he pulled the window shut behind him and returned to the public bar. Naturally enough the other two villains had made good their escape.

'Did you catch the varmint?' the landlady demanded to know. This hardly required an answer as it was obvious he hadn't.

'No, he got away. Another constable is in pursuit.' He touched his hat and dashed out to join in the hue and cry. He was about to set off when he noticed something in the shadows by the wall. It was the cash box and unopened. This wasn't going to be quite such a disaster as he had feared. He snatched up the box and tucked it under his arm. It would be returned to the landlady intact, but at the moment it was crucial evidence.

He wondered if Fred had managed to apprehend the cove what had shimmied down the drainpipe. He completed his beat up to the point he passed the station and then bounded up the steps.

He put the cash box on the counter. 'Didn't catch the bugger what dropped this. Did Fred bring him in, Sarge?'

'No, he must have scarpered. Where's this been nicked from?'

Alfie quickly explained the circumstances and the evidence was logged. He returned to his duty and the remainder of the night was uneventful. Fred was waiting for him by the coffee stall.

'I know who the bugger was but he showed me a clean pair of heels. At least he didn't get away with the cash.'

'I'm to return it tonight. I ain't too keen on scrambling over roofs and suchlike, don't have much of a head for heights.'

'Nor me. I'm going to get something to eat and then off to my bed. I'll be glad when the weather improves – bleedin' cold out here in the winter.'

Their usual pies were waiting on the counter and they wolfed them down. He still missed Buster, especially at times like this. Fred enquired after his application to join the detective branch at Scotland Yard.

'You heard anything, Alfie?'

'Didn't expect to. Me name's down. If there's a vacancy, I might be lucky. There's got to be a better way of stopping the criminals than chasing after them once they've got the stuff.'

He could hardly tell his friend that he knew exactly how the system worked from first-hand experience, that anything stolen would be handed on, and the person they were chasing would be empty-handed if he was caught.

* * *

Chelmsford, April 1849

The weather continued to improve, as did the business. Sarah had now had time to study the lease in detail and was confident she hadn't signed a document she couldn't deal with. Davie had left home and was happily lodging with his master, which gave her an excuse to be out in the afternoon, with Betty and the children, two or three times a week in order to visit him.

They were returning from an afternoon away in good spirits when a hired carriage pulled up in front of the shop. They were still some distance from their home and Sarah hastily pulled the children and her friend into the concealment of a carriage archway. From their hiding place they watched Hatch kick down the steps and then hand her mother down to the pavement.

'I knew it. My mother has been more secretive than usual lately. When she went out this morning she was wearing an outfit I've not seen before. She has married that monster despite both of us telling her of his true character.'

'Hardly surprising we were not invited to the wedding ceremony – if there has in fact been one,' Betty replied.

'From the predatory smile on that man's face I'm certain he's now the owner of our business. We cannot continue to lurk here; we must make a show of being happy for them.'

Even as she spoke the words Sarah knew that it was possible she'd left their escape too late. Their new home was in the process of being redecorated and furnished for their arrival. She'd thought they would have longer before Ma married that man.

'It's going to be more difficult to leave now he's in residence. We certainly won't be able to take more than the clothes we stand up in when we do go. I thank the Lord I've not told the little ones – at least we know they'll not blurt out our intentions.'

The happy couple had now gone inside and, as always, they intended to enter through the side gate. However, when she attempted to open it the gate refused to budge.

'This is never bolted on the inside until the night-time. Unless we're prepared to walk around to the garden gate we've no option but to go in the front.'

Betty nodded. 'This has been planned whilst we've been out. I doubt we'll find a locked gate is the only thing that has changed.'

The front door was also locked and Sarah was obliged to knock as if she were a visitor and not a resident. A few moments later the door was opened with due ceremony, and an unknown maidservant, dressed in black uniform with a smart white cap and apron, curtsied.

'The master and mistress are waiting to speak to you in the drawing room if you would care to come this way.'

Drawing room? As far as Sarah was concerned they only had a front parlour – nothing so grand as a drawing room. Betty was carrying Jimmy who had refused to walk the last few hundred yards and Tommy and Mary were hanging back unsure of what was happening.

Sarah returned to reassure them but the girl intervened. 'The children are to come with me, Mrs Cooper. They are not allowed in this part of the house. They must remain upstairs or in the kitchen.'

There was little point in arguing with the servant – the girl had been given instructions and was merely doing her duty. She turned and spoke softly to her friend, making sure her words were not overheard. 'Betty, you go with them. I fear we'll find things arranged differently upstairs. We shall remain dignified and leave here tomorrow.'

'Understood. We shall consider ourselves the heroines of a romantic novel held prisoner by a dastardly villain. Good luck.'

Betty dashed off obviously happy not to be the one obliged to go in and speak to Hatch and his new wife. This was a second betrayal. In future she had no mother – the woman she was about to speak to was a stranger to her.

She marched into the newly designated drawing room with her head held high. The newlyweds were standing side by side dressed in their finery. If she hadn't been expecting this to happen, she might have been overwhelmed. As it was she was pleased to see it was they who looked disconcerted.

She raked them from head to toe as if examining something unpleasant. Hatch and his wife exchanged a glance. She had wrong-footed them and was glad. Tomorrow they would leave, so today she would speak the truth.

'I shall not offer you my congratulations. What I will say is that I consider you a well-matched couple and hope that you both get the life that you deserve.'

Hatch wasn't a tall man, but he was impressively broad. As she watched, his face turned an unbecoming shade of red and his carefully waxed moustache positively vibrated with fury. Her mother's expression of smug satisfaction vanished and for a second Sarah wished she had been more conciliatory.

Then he moved forward with such speed she had no time to take avoiding action. His fist crashed into her temple. There was a moment's blinding pain and she was falling backwards. As if from a distance she heard someone scream, a man shout, and then her head spun and her world went black.

11

Sarah came around lying on the floor, but beneath her questing fingers were bare boards. She wasn't in the front parlour where she'd fallen or indeed her own bedchamber. Then Betty's anxious face swam into view.

'Thank the good Lord you've woken up. I thought he'd killed you and so did your ma.'

The wave of nausea that engulfed her made a response impossible. Her friend supported her head as she retched into a bowl. When this was over she couldn't remain conscious and everything blurred for a second time.

When she came around again she was in bed, but it wasn't her own; it was hard and narrow. She didn't make the mistake of opening her eyes too quickly, but lay immobile trying to get her bearings without aggravating the appalling headache and sickness.

It was dark; wherever she was it was cold, but not unpleasantly so. There was the murmur of voices and she listened carefully trying to recognise the speakers.

'He can't be allowed to get away with it. You should call the constable and have him arrested, Auntie Betty.'

This was Davie's voice. Then her friend replied.

'I didn't want to do anything until Sarah's well enough to say what she wants. We're leaving here as soon as she's better; the physician said it's a nasty concussion but she should be on her feet in a few days.'

Sarah risked opening her eyes and thought she could probably join in the conversation without aggravating her condition. 'Don't involve the police, Betty. It might make things harder for us to go.'

Her friend rushed to her side. 'Do you want anything to drink? The doctor said you must keep your fluids up.'

'Nothing, I feel too sick. Where are we?'

'That man sacked our girls and employed his own staff and they rearranged everything whilst we were out. They've put the little ones in the attics and we've got the box room.'

'It's not for long. He can't keep us locked up – we're not prisoners. Don't make a fuss about our accommodation. Davie, please say nothing of this to anyone. Do I have your word?'

He took her hand and squeezed it. 'I promise, Ma. We'll say it's a fall.'

Talking had exhausted her and she drifted off into a semiconscious state once more. It was dark when she roused and her need was desperate.

'Betty, I need the chamber pot.'

There was the sound of bedcovers being thrown back and then the necessary item arrived in the nick of time. Sitting up to use this had not been as unpleasant as she'd expected. She still had a horrible headache but believed she was no longer in imminent danger of casting up her accounts.

'Can you light a candle, Betty? We need to talk.'

* * *

Whitechapel, April 1849

Alfie escorted his half a dozen prisoners to the magistrates' court, said his piece, and was then free until the following morning when he began his rota of daytime duties. It had been a busy night. There had been a right old punch-up, knuckledusters, stiletto knives, the lot, down by the docks between a group of Irish labourers and the seaman from a foreign ship. It had taken a dozen constables to stop the fisticuffs.

No one seemed to know what had started it and there was no hard feelings between the participants in the cold light of day. The foreigners was put back on board their ship and told to stay there and the Irish was bound over and threatened with jail if they offended again.

On his return to the station to complete his paperwork he was greeted with enthusiasm by the sergeant on duty. 'At last, Nightingale. How many bleeders were there at court today?'

'Too many, Sarge. Somethink up?'

'Message came from Scotland Yard – you're to report to Inspector Burgess first thing. He don't like to be kept waiting, so you'd better get a move on.'

Police constables were to conduct themselves with decorum at all times, but Alfie ignored that instruction and tore down Leman Street and into Whitechapel Road where there was more chance of catching a hackney carriage to take him to Scotland Yard. Despite the fact the streets were filling up with early morning hawkers and traders, he made excellent time and he arrived just as a nearby church clock struck nine.

Was this the opportunity he was waiting for? Had he reached the top of the list and was going to be offered a position as a detective? He paid the exorbitant fare with good grace – sometimes it were worth it to spend hard-earned rhino on what might be thought of as a luxury.

He had ample opportunity to polish his boots on the rag he kept in his pocket during the long drive. He'd also smoothed out the fingermarks on the fur of his topper. His brass buttons was polished, his face clean-shaven – he couldn't do any more to improve his appearance.

He enquired at the desk for Inspector Burgess and was told to make his way to an office on the first floor. The door was half glazed. He could see the inspector sitting at his desk through the pebbled glass. He took a steadying breath, knocked, and was told to enter.

Alfie saluted and clicked his heels together as if he were a soldier. 'Constable Nightingale, reporting for duty, sir.'

The inspector raised a bushy eyebrow but otherwise ignored his formality. He gestured to a chair in front of the desk. 'Come in, young man. I've work for you. Seat yourself and hear what it is I wish you to do. This is by way of a test, Nightingale. Depending on your conduct you could be offered a permanent position here working directly for me.'

'I'll not let you down, Inspector.'

The fact that he'd just finished a twelve-hour shift, had eaten nothing for hours, and was in desperate need of a bit of shut-eye was forgotten. He was being given the opportunity he'd prayed for. Nothing was going to get in the way of him becoming a member of the CID.

* * *

Chelmsford, April 1849

'The three girls who were dismissed – do you know where they are now?' Sarah asked Betty.

'Sally, the one who's been doing the cooking, comes from around here somewhere and I think they've all gone there temporarily.'

'Is Davie still here?' He obviously wasn't in the room with them but it was possible he'd decided to stay and was sleeping with John and the children in the attic.

'He's a good boy. The little ones didn't want to go upstairs on their own and I didn't like to leave you, so he's up there with them. Shall I fetch him?'

'Yes, I need him to go around to Sally's house and offer those three employment with us in Colchester. There's sufficient money in my purse for their train fares and some over for them to buy what they will need until we get there.'

Betty understood what she was planning. 'You're going to ask them to get on with the cleaning and such so it's ready when we go? They'll be that grateful to have employment they'll not cavil at leaving Chelmsford. Which reminds me, what about the girls in the workshop? Have you spoken to them about coming with us?'

'I have, and three of them agreed. They weren't taken on by my mother so have no loyalty to her.'

Her head was now aching abominably and her stomach turning over unpleasantly. She hastily lay flat and closed her eyes. 'I'm not feeling too clever. I'll have to leave everything to you until I'm on my feet again. I think if you exaggerate how bad I am that man will stay away from all of us. The last thing he wants is for the law to be involved.'

'Shall I send John to school as usual tomorrow?'

'Yes, I don't want our plans to be known. Hopefully, we can leave at the end of the week.'

Sarah drifted off to sleep, confident her son and her friend would deal with everything until she was able to take control again. Spot was going to live with Davie in future as he was no longer allowed even in the scullery by the new regime.

When Alfie and Robert eventually returned they would deal with Hatch – he would get his comeuppance and quite possibly her traitorous mother would find herself a widow for the third time.

The next two days were spent resting, giving herself time to recover from the concussion. Betty had shown her the hideous bruise on her forehead and she had been shocked.

'No one could possibly think this was caused by my falling downstairs. I've got a bonnet that has a deep brim and if you added some net it would hide my face completely. I've no wish to travel on the train looking as I do.'

'You'll be pleased to know the seamstresses have already left and gone to join Sally and the other two in Colchester. Mrs Rand, no Mrs Hatch, is beside herself. I think she's already regretting her actions. That man is lording it over everyone and the servants he's taken on act as if they're waiting on gentry, not an ordinary criminal from Colchester.'

'Don't let it upset you, Betty. Do as he wants without complaint, but continue to protest that I'm not recovering and you're going to call in the doctor again. That should keep Hatch quiet. If he thinks I'm likely to die and make him a murderer he'll keep out of our way.

'I'm surprised my mother hasn't come up to see how I am for herself. She's not a bad woman, just gullible.'

'He won't let her. He's taken over your office and is issuing orders as if he knows what he's talking about. It's a good thing you've already taken your patterns and such, because you'd never get them now.'

'Hatch's in for a rude awakening when he discovers that the success of the business rests mainly on my input. My mother isn't as adept as I at cutting. The customers who return do so because of me. I wonder if they might be persuaded to catch the train to Colchester?'

Betty laughed. 'Not likely, not when there's such a long walk from the station. There aren't any places making ready-made children's clothes in Colchester. Does Mr Hyam make women's clothes as well as men's?'

'He might be now, but he certainly wasn't when we left two years ago. I won't be able to compete on price if he is, but I can offer a more personal service and take in, turn up or let out garments when necessary.'

A week after she'd been so brutally attacked Sarah thought she was well enough to leave. The house was locked up every night and the keys kept by Hatch. John was now forced to leave by the garden gate, which had no key but was bolted on the inside. This was the way they would escape.

Fortunately, the weather was clement; carrying heavy carpetbags in the rain would have made things so much more difficult. At dawn Betty slipped upstairs and with John quickly dressed the children who were beside themselves with excitement at this unusual occurrence.

It grieved Sarah to be leaving so many of her possessions behind but they could eventually be replaced – family was more important and hers would be coming with her to start a new life. All they had to do was creep through the house without disturbing the new owner, or his minions, and leave via the garden gate to catch the early morning train.

John had gone down first and quietly opened the back door. Betty had followed carrying Tommy, with Jimmy and Mary close behind her. She was still finding being upright made her dizzy so she was bringing up the rear, using the walls to keep straight.

She was steps from the door when Hatch, with a roar of rage, appeared behind her.

'Not so fast, you conniving bitch. Your snivelling brats are welcome to go, but you're stopping here. I own you now, and you're going to work for me whether you likes it or not.'

Her head was spinning but somehow she increased her pace and threw herself at the door. He moved much faster than she did and grabbed her by the shoulders slamming her hard against the wall. As he reached round to close the door, to trap her inside, something large and white hurled itself into the opening.

Spot, snarling ferociously, attached himself to Hatch's arm and the man's screams of agony echoed through the house. No chance of a silent escape now. Davie appeared and grabbed her, yanking her outside.

'Quick, Ma, go with the others. Spot and I will deal with this bastard.'

She didn't stop to argue but did as she was bid. Davie was a man now and quite capable of taking care of himself. Betty was waiting by the open garden gate, the children wide-eyed but not particularly upset, which was a good thing.

'Is Spot killing that horrible man, Ma?' Mary asked.

'It would serve him right if he did, but no, the dog was just protecting me. Look, Davie and Spot are coming now.'

'There's blood dripping from his jaws, Auntie Sarah,' Jimmy said gleefully.

'I can see that. I'm sure he'll clean himself up. We have a train to catch so let's not dawdle here.'

The cat, which was being carried in a burlap sack by Betty, was protesting loudly at all the rushing about.

'Smoke, settle down, there's a good pussycat. No one's going to hurt you,' Betty said soothingly.

At any moment Sarah expected one of Hatch's minions to step out from a side street and prevent them from catching the train.

'Davie, we'd better take the dog with us. Hatch will kill Spot if he can get his hands on him.'

'I reckon you're right, Ma. He'd be better off in Colchester protecting you. Hatch might be here, but there's going to be coves what used to work for him living there.'

'He's just like Buster; Uncle Alfie told us how his dog protected him many a time,' John chipped in.

'Have you got him secure on his rope, John?' Sarah was relieved to see the dog had licked his chops clean and now looked like a docile family pet.

Betty and the children were laughing and talking as if nothing untoward had taken place. Could they not see leaving Chelmsford might not be the safe option they'd hoped for? Davie was right to point out there could well be villains on Hatch's payroll prepared to take revenge in any way possible.

Somehow, she pinned on a bright smile and joined in the jolly chatter. She embraced Davie and he ran off to work. She bought the tickets but didn't relax until the train steamed out of the station with all of them safely aboard.

At this time of the morning they had the compartment to themselves, which meant when Spot broke wind noisily no one else was offended. The children thought this hilarious but she and Betty were less impressed by the noxious smell.

When they disembarked she gathered them together. 'Our new home is number sixty on North Hill. The shop I have bought used to be owned by someone called Nightingale. Isn't that interesting?'

'Cor, that's grand, Auntie Sarah,' Tommy said as he hopped from one foot to the other eager to go and see this marvel for himself.

'Where will we be going to school next year, Ma?' Mary asked. Her daughter had her priorities in order.

'That's yet to be decided, love. First, we have to get settled and find a place for John. There's a good school in Crouch Street for boys but that might well be too expensive at the moment.'

'It don't make no never mind to me, Ma, if I ain't at school. I know me letters and can figure all right – a lot better than most boys my age.'

'We don't have to worry about that for the moment, John. I'm sure there'll be plenty to keep you busy. There's the dog to walk twice a day now and that's your job.'

The walk from the station to their new home was accomplished without further excitement. Apart from several curious glances in her direction because her face was obscured behind the netting on her bonnet, they drew no more attention than one would expect at that time of the morning.

She led them under the archway to the side gate. The cobbles had been swept, fresh paintwork gleaned everywhere and the windows were sparkling – quite different from her previous visit.

The gate was opened before she had the opportunity to knock. 'Mrs Cooper, we didn't expect you until the weekend. Mr Daniel delivered the furniture and it looks a treat.' Sally ushered them in as proud of the house as if she were personally responsible for the improvements.

'Have you and the other girls everything you need?'

'We have, madam, lovely and cosy we are up in them attics. I wasn't sure if you wanted me to carry on as your cook, but I'm happy to do so. Nothing I like better than being in the kitchen.'

'Then in future you will be referred to as Cook – not Sally. Once we're settled I'll try and find you a room of your own. I'll also increase your wages.'

'That'll be grand, but I'm happy enough sharing for the moment.'

Betty and the others were wandering about exclaiming in delight at the improvements. Mr Daniel, the man who'd bought Alfie's business a couple of years ago, had returned all the furniture her brother and Betty had been obliged to leave behind when they'd run away to Chelmsford.

There were even rugs on the floor, the fires were lit in the front parlour and there were sufficient chairs in the kitchen around the table to seat everyone. She put her worries to one side and enjoyed the splendour of her new home.

'Betty, will you show the children where they'll be sleeping? I think you could put the cat down. I don't think he'll run away as long as we're all here.'

'I'll get a dirt tray sorted, Ma, so he won't mess in the house,' John said helpfully.

'Thank you, son. I'm going into the workshop. I won't be long.'

Things in here were as well organised as everywhere else and the three girls she'd brought with her had already started on the vital replacements the entire family would need as they'd been forced to abandon all their clothes in Chelmsford.

Doris, the oldest of the three and their spokesperson, looked up as she walked in. 'Pleased to see you, Mrs Cooper. We've got petticoats, drawers and such finished for all of you but don't have the wherewithal to make anything else. Do you have a wholesaler I can visit?'

'I'm going to the factory in Queen Street later. They are bound to have some offcuts we can use for the children. My intention is to go to London and visit the warehouses personally as soon as we're settled. I'd hoped to do so before we came but – well, as you can see things didn't go as well as we'd hoped.' As she spoke she removed her bonnet and there was an audible gasp from the girls.

'As I explained to you all, I can't afford to pay you until the business is up and running, but you have your board and lodging free and I will make it up to you as soon as I can.'

The girls nodded. 'We know you will, Mrs Cooper, don't you worry yourself. We're happy to work for nothing until things pick up.'

12

WHITECHAPEL, MAY 1849

'I wish you to accompany me to Ascot. Do you have civilian garments that will pass muster at such a place?' Inspector Burgess enquired of Alfie.

'I do, sir. I ain't going to look out of place amongst the toffs.'

The inspector smiled. 'You'll have to keep your trap shut or improve your diction, Nightingale.'

'I can do that, Inspector Burgess. I can assure you that I can speak as well as the next man if needs be.' Alfie hoped his attempt at sounding grand would be enough to satisfy his new superior.

'Excellent. Remain in your lodgings for now. You are on secondment to me, not permanently transferred. Get home and change then present yourself at Waterloo Station. We shall be catching the midday train, so you had better hurry if you are not to miss it.'

It were a bloody long way from Scotland Yard back to Leman Street and then almost as far to get back to the station. It was as if the inspector had deliberately set out to make life difficult for him – this message could have been left with the sergeant and saved a great deal of time and expense.

No point in moaning – he'd better do as he was bid if he wanted to join the CID after this excursion. He'd never been to a racecourse of any sort. It were a pastime for the rich, not folk like him. God knows why the inspector wanted him in plain clothes. There must be something going on where a uniformed constable couldn't be employed.

He asked the jarvey to wait for him whilst he changed. If he hadn't had the foresight to do so he would have missed the train. As it was, he was obliged to dodge past the ticket collector and leap on the train without having first purchased a ticket. Now all he had to do was make his way down the platform on the next halt until he discovered the inspector. It were likely he would be in first class, certainly not in third where he were now.

First class, for the gents, would be at the front of the train and he'd jumped on at the back. He would have to get out at the next stop and hope he could reach the required carriage before the train pulled out again. The inspector would think he'd missed the train – nothing he could do about that now.

He was ready and had the door open before the train was stationary. A guard saw him racing along the platform and ran ahead to open the door to a first-class carriage. 'Here you are, sir, not the first gentleman to have had to change carriages.'

Alfie nodded but had the sense to keep his trap shut. The door banged behind him. This compartment were empty – too much to hope he'd get in the right one first off. At the next station he hadn't far to go as the inspector were in the adjacent compartment. Instead of greeting him with a scowl, he laughed.

'Well done, Nightingale. I didn't think you'd make it. Here, let me see you. Yes, you will do very nicely.' He waved to the seat opposite him and gratefully Alfie took it. All this dashing about with no sleep and nothing to eat had exhausted him.

'I'll make it brief, then you can rest until we get there. I'm well aware you've just come off night duty.'

Alfie could hardly believe his ears when he heard why they were going to the races. Some toff, Lord Fonsby, what was a close friend of the chief constable, had demanded that his runners were guarded from the nobblers. But not by ordinary peelers, no, he insisted this work had to be done by plain-clothes men.

'Surely, sir, seeing uniforms would be a better deterrent than having a couple of coves hanging about?'

'Exactly what I told the chief constable. It would seem his lordship suspects a friend of the family of skulduggery. He wishes us to apprehend him, not scare him away.'

'That's all fine and dandy, but why must you come? Could they not have used another detective?'

'I am to pretend I am a potential buyer of one of his horses. You are to be my man of affairs.'

Alfie couldn't hold back his snort of laughter. 'I know bugger all about such things, sir. But, not to worry, I'm looking forward to the play-acting.'

He enjoyed the novelty of travelling in style, although he were familiar with trains in general. There was things he wanted to know but the inspector had told him to sleep and that were probably the best idea. He was awoken by a buffet on the shoulder that almost sent him from his seat.

'We are here, Nightingale. Remember, you must address me as sir or Mr Burgess, not by my rank. I expect you were wondering whether we are to stay overnight and if so whereabouts.'

'I were – I was indeed, wishing to know that, sir.'

'We shall return on the last train. During race week they run until midnight. There won't be time for you to return to your lodgings so I have arranged for you to stay with me. I am unmarried so your arrival won't be upsetting any wife.'

If he'd known he would have brought a clean collar and his shaving gear. He must hope that these things would be made available to him otherwise he would look out of place mixing with the toffs tomorrow.

On the short walk to the racecourse he had ample time to assess the folk who were also making their way on foot to the venue. They were a mixed bunch, some smartly dressed as they were, others middling folk who'd come for a day out.

He tried to look as if he were comfortable in his surroundings, to not gawp at the things he saw. But he were amazed at the betting booths, what was numerous. They were tents, not permanent like, but fitted up smart inside. The grass were covered with carpet and there were wine for anyone what went in on a wooden sideboard.

Men in smart livery stood at the entrances calling out for the unwary to go in and play roulette or some such thing. As they shouted they drew back the curtain a little so those outside could see what they were missing.

They were heading for the stables, but everything stopped when the young queen were driven past. She were attended by the royal huntsmen what came in front and the inspector told him the other coves were the knights of Windsor and ministers in special costume. She were a lovely girl and he were proud to be a subject.

The course itself were quite clear – only them what was special were allowed to wander on that turf. Everywhere he looked there was carriages with the toffs and their ladies filling them. It were the grandest scene but there were still thieves around even in such a place.

'Look at that, sir. Shall I go after him?' Alfie had just seen someone lift a gold pocket watch and hand it back to his accomplice.

'No, we must make our way immediately to where the horses are being kept. Lord Fonsby is a tall, thin fellow with mutton-chop whiskers and pale blue eyes.'

As Alfie didn't expect to be introduced to this aristocrat he thought the description unnecessary. They were now approaching the temporary stables and there were an overwhelming smell of horse shit. This didn't seem to be putting the gents off as they were strolling up and down examining the racehorses and discussing in loud voices whether they were going to put money on the nag or not.

'See that dark bay – the one with barred teeth and ears back – that's his lordship's stallion. Nasty bugger. Watch you don't get bitten. The chestnut on the right is his stablemate, comes to keep him company but doesn't race. The grey mare on the left is favourite to win at least two big races this week.'

'What about the stallion?'

'He's unpredictable – is as likely to toss his jockey over the fence as complete the race. If things go well there's not a horse can catch him. Winning will double his stud fees at least.'

Alfie was glad he didn't have to get too close to the animals. He weren't that fond of horses. His job was to walk along behind the inspector pretending to take notes. In fact, he might as well take actual notes; they could come in useful if anyone were ever caught for nobbling horses.

His lordship didn't make an appearance but his trainer did. Alfie remained a discreet distance behind the two men whilst they were supposedly talking about buying into the stallion or the mare. It would seem that often gents owned part of the horse, a consortium like, what shared expenses and prizes. Some toffs did this just so they could parade around in the owners' area before and after the race. He knew this because the inspector had filled him in.

The racing drew to a close and the inspector said he was joining his lordship for supper and drinks. 'Here's your ticket for the train, Nightingale. I'll see you at the station at midnight.'

What the bleedin' hell he were supposed to do for the next few hours Alfie had no idea. He'd bought a couple of pasties and coffee earlier so wouldn't starve to death. He walked over to the stables and came to a sudden decision. Surely now was the perfect time for anyone who wished to interfere with the horses to do it? He would hide with the mare – he weren't going nowhere near the stallion, that were for sure.

The grey seemed unbothered by his appearance in her stall. 'Move over, gal, let a fellow find a seat, why don't you?' He patted her neck and she stepped to one side allowing him a comfortable spot underneath the manger and out of sight of anyone what happened to glance in.

There was the welcome, and reassuring weight, of the shooter he had been issued with resting on his thigh. The inspector had handed it over without enquiring if Alfie knew how to use it nor having commented on why he thought the weapon necessary.

It were warm and comfortable hunched down in the corner and the thoroughbred mare appeared to enjoy his company as she frequently lowered her head and nudged him. It had been dark for an hour when he heard footsteps approaching. Slowly he tipped himself onto his knees and withdrew his pistol.

Then he heard whispering outside but it were too quiet for him to pick out what were being said. Then whoever it was moved closer.

'It seems a shame to poison such a beautiful animal. Are you quite sure Lord Fonsby requires us to do so?'

The speaker was a gent – not some ruffian as he'd expected. His companion replied.

'The horse has thrown a splint, won't be able to race. He's bet heavily on the outcome. This way he'll be recompensed with the insurance payment.'

How the hell were these buggers going to kill the horse without attracting the attention of the night watch what patrolled the area on a regular basis? The animal shifted nervously and snuffled against his shoulder. He patted her and she calmed. Whatever this splint was, the mare would be able to breed even if she couldn't race. No one was going to kill her on his watch.

He flattened himself in the darkness and waited.

'Dammit! Silver Star's not turned round to greet us as she usually does.' The speaker made encouraging noises but Silver Star kept her rump firmly to them. 'I shall have to go into the stable to feed her the apple. Keep watch – let me know if anyone is approaching.'

Alfie had no intention of firing his gun. Not only would killing a toff cause problems for himself and inspector, the noise would terrify the horses. He would use it as a club. He'd knock the bugger senseless and then deal with his companion in a similar fashion.

The fact that the very man who'd employed them to guard his horses was behind this attack was something his superiors could deal with.

The first man, the one with the poisoned apple, slid into the stall talking softly to the horse. Alfie moved silently through the straw and hit the man on the back of the head. He crumpled without making a sound. Silver Star put her head down to investigate and to his horror she found the apple. He kicked it into the straw under the manger not a moment too soon.

He had a piece of bread left over from his tea and he handed this to the horse. She crunched into it with gusto. The man outside must believe the mare was eating the lethal fruit. Alfie could see nothing. He kept his hand on the horse's flank and used this to guide him to the exit.

He crouched, knowing that whoever was outside would be looking at head height. This should be sufficient to keep him invisible until he'd taken care of him. He threw himself out onto the path and his shoulder collided with the legs of the waiting gent.

His sudden appearance gave him the advantage and with scarcely a sound he knocked the other cove out. He'd had the foresight to bring several lengths of twine with him – bulky handcuffs would have been visible in his smart jacket pockets.

He dragged the unconscious man into the stall and tied his hands and feet. He then did the same for the first person. He tore his only good handkerchief in half and stuffed a piece in each of their gobs.

'Don't step on them, girl. I'll not be long.'

Inspector Burgess would be dining somewhere in the fine new grandstand. He needed to speak to him urgently. He ran to the nearest gaslight and brushed down his clothes and restored the shine to his boots. If he was to get in and find his inspector he needed to look smart and keep his mouth shut.

He thought he might be stopped from entering, but the doorman waved him through as if he belonged there. 'I am looking for Lord Fonsby's party. Would you be good enough to direct me to them?'

Alfie thought he sounded stilted and strange but the uniformed flunky nodded.

'His lordship is entertaining in the third reception room. Follow this corridor and you will find it, sir.'

Alfie didn't risk speaking again and possibly revealing who he really was. He nodded and strode off expecting to be revealed as an impostor at any moment. He found the room and from the racket inside, they were all drunk. Less chance of him being stopped if their senses were impaired.

He pushed open the door. The air was blue with cigar smoke and smelled little better than a common beerhouse. He remained just inside the door whilst he scanned the dozen or so gentlemen looking for his inspector.

'Outside, Nightingale, we can't talk in here.'

His superior took his arm and almost bundled him out. 'Come with me, sir. I'll explain on the way. I'm buggered if I know what to do next.' He quickly described what had happened and his inspector was as shocked as he'd been.

'This is an unmitigated disaster. We've been dragged into something nasty. His lordship was well aware that if he was discovered we could do little about it. If the horse died then he would let the world know two of Scotland Yard's finest were in charge, that he'd taken every precaution, and the insurance company would have had no option but to pay up.'

'I don't reckon the night watch will have discovered anything. I was thinking, them stable hands what look after the horses wouldn't be too pleased that someone had tried to poison one of them.'

'I get your drift, Nightingale. Find them and have them raise the alarm themselves. I think the best thing we can do is scuttle back to Town. Better to be as far away as possible when word of this attempted fraud becomes common knowledge.'

'I'll see you at the station, sir. I take it we don't have to return here tomorrow?'

'Unfortunately, we must. I intend to plead ignorance, and you must do the same. God knows how Fonsby will wriggle out of this one, but he's an aristocrat so I can't see him coming before the magistrates.'

Alfie found not only the two stable hands but also the jockey and told them what had taken place. They were incensed and delighted to take the credit for catching the two would-be horse murderers. He sloped off into the darkness and left them to it.

He soon caught up with his inspector who did not walk as fast as he did. 'There's an excellent hostelry adjacent to the station. I think we should catch the train we intended so as not to arouse any suspicions. I shall treat you to a blowout. You deserve to eat and drink your fill tonight. I am well satisfied with your conduct. I shall recommend that you are transferred immediately to Scotland Yard.'

13

COLCHESTER, JULY 1849

Sarah put down her scissors and straightened, then rubbed her back and rolled her shoulders a few times. Cutting patterns was hard work at the best of times but in this heat she was finding it unusually difficult.

John had not enrolled at the school in Crouch Street but decided he was going to become her apprentice and then he could run the business when she retired. She wasn't sure being a tailor was a good option as so much work was given to women to do at home.

'Ma, Mrs Billings has come to see you. Shall I bring her through?'

'No, John, I'm done here for the day. Don't forget you have to go down to the station and collect a delivery in an hour.'

'I'm going now. Can I take Tommy with me as he just loves to ride on the barrow?'

'Ask Auntie Betty, but I've no objection.'

Her three girls had now increased to four to cope with the demand. She rather thought that buying her materials in London and offering the latest fashions was the reason that her business was so successful. She had been asked if she intended to make corsets but these were best left to the experts. The fashion for the well-off ladies meant they had to have nipped-in waists, which could only be achieved by lacing.

Coming from a working family she had never bothered to wear a corset and had no intention of doing so now. She preferred to be able to breathe freely and move about without restriction. Everything had gone as she'd hoped – there'd been no trouble from any of Hatch's ex-minions and she was building up a healthy bank balance.

Robert and Joe should have been back last month and she was becoming increasingly worried about the safety of both of them. There had been no further correspondence either, which was definitely a concern. Perhaps Ada had come with some good news, but she doubted her future mother-in-law would hear from Robert before her.

She stopped to look in the kitchen, which was now greatly improved and spotlessly clean. 'I should like a tray of tea and whatever has just been baked, which smells so delicious. Please bring it to the front parlour.'

The three girls who had been sacked by Hatch had become, like the four who sewed in the workshop, part of the family. Sally remained in charge of the kitchen and the other two worked not only as maids but also as shop assistants. As she had two women coming in three times a week to do the laundry and heavy work her girls were not overtaxed.

'Ada, I'm so glad to see you. Have you news for me?'

Her friend dabbed her eyes. 'Not good news, Sarah love, I'm afraid. One of my boys, the one who works on the trains, managed to get to the docks and speak to the harbour master. There has been no sighting of *The Empress* since last year. It's been written up as lost, and all hands with it.'

Sarah's knees buckled, and she collapsed into the nearest chair. 'I can't believe both of them have gone. I feared as much when we heard nothing, but have been praying nightly that somehow they will find their way back to us.'

'I'm not giving up hope, Sarah love, not until next year. Robert told me once about a ship that was blown off course by a tropical storm and was wrecked on rocks close to shore. Most of the crew and passengers were able to wade to the beach. Unfortunately, they were in a part of the world inhabited by savages, wild animals and dangerous insects. By the time a passing fisherman discovered them half had died.'

'How is that a cheerful tale?'

'The other half eventually found their way back home, but almost two years had passed since the ship had sunk and the families had given them up for dead.'

'So, it is not entirely impossible that they might be safe on some deserted shore but unable to get home? I shall keep that thought in my heart and not despair. I'll not mention it to John, Davie or the children.'

The tea tray arrived and they talked of other things. 'Ada, I know you rely on Robert's support. How long will the company continue to pay his wages?'

'That's the problem, Sarah. I didn't like to say so but they've written to say that they will cease paying in December and consider him dead. I shall receive a lump sum as compensation, but that's all.'

'Surely you have no debts to worry about? You only have three children not working – the others must be able to help out if necessary.' Sarah leant over and patted her friend on the arm. 'This is a big house. If ever you need to, you can move in here with us.'

'I hope it won't come to that. Something I never told you is that the house is rented. Robert always said he would buy it, but never got around to doing so. The landlord wants the house for his daughter and son-in-law, especially now it's in such good condition. He puts the rent up every few months in the hope that I'll be forced to move. He wouldn't do so if Robert was here.'

'Then you must move immediately. I'm certain that Robert would wish us all to live together when we marry so why not do so now? As far as I'm concerned, you're my mother-in-law already.'

* * *

London, July 1849

Alfie tried to look professional, to not show his joy, but failed dismally. It was truly a night of celebration and he began to think that he would be reunited with his family in a few months – that's if Betty still wanted him. If she didn't, he would understand, and do everything he could to support her and the boys and see they didn't make the mistakes he had.

Robert should be back from his travels now and he reckoned he and

Sarah would tie the knot and move back to Colchester. They'd not live in the same neighbourhood he had; they'd go somewhere grand, so there was little likelihood of that bastard Hatch even knowing she was there. After all, she wouldn't be Mrs Cooper but Mrs Billings.

After several beers and a feast of mutton chops, beef puddings and apple pie, he were stuffed full and so happy he were likely to burst into song if he weren't careful. The housekeeper was no doubt in her bed when they eventually arrived at the inspector's home.

'Quietly now, young man – I don't want to wake my staff.' He stopped and pointed to a closed door. 'This is your room for the night. You'll find everything you want on the nightstand. I'll bring you a clean collar and cuffs in the morning. Well done, Nightingale, well done indeed. A good night's work and we've kept the chief constable out of it.'

This was a modest house, not as large as the one that his ma had in Chelmsford, but it were in a smart residential area with trees and such, and no filth in the gutters neither. The street was well lit and all the detached dwellings was of recent construction.

Maybe he could buy something similar for his own family if he worked hard and got promoted to inspector one day? He hung his smart clothes up, didn't drop them on the floor as he usually did in his lodgings. He didn't want his superior coming in and thinking he didn't know how to behave.

There was cold water in the jug and a towel waiting on the stand. He stripped to his skin and washed from top to bottom and then shaved – he didn't want the whiff of the stables to follow him about tomorrow. There was no nightshirt – but why should there be? He tumbled into bed naked and was instantly asleep.

There was a soft tap on the door the next morning and he pushed himself up onto his elbows and called that whoever it was should come in. As the doors opened he recalled he hadn't a stitch on and hastily pulled the sheet under his chin.

A woman of middling years, faded brown hair, and lace cap, stepped in with a tray. 'Good morning, Mr Nightingale, I thought you might like a nice cup of tea before you get up. The master has asked me to give you these as well.'

She put down the tray on a small table within reach of the bed and then carefully placed the collar and cuffs on the chair with his neatly folded shirt.

'Is the inspector waiting for me?'

'Good heavens, no, he is still fast asleep in bed.' She smiled and her plain face became pretty. 'I thought you would like to be downstairs, ready and waiting when he comes down for breakfast. It always helps to make a good impression, don't you think?'

'It do indeed. I can't remember ever having tea in bed – I thank you for your consideration. I shall be down soon. I'll bring me own slops...'

'You shall do no such thing, young man. I have a girl who takes care of that.'

She smiled again and whisked from the room. He wondered if his inspector made a habit of bringing home stray constables or if this were unusual?

He'd like to think he was a cut above the others – not many of them had as many arrests to their name as he did. He would have to purchase himself some new togs if he were to be a plain-clothes detective. Constables got two outfits a year provided – he wondered if there was an allowance given to detectives. He blooming well hoped so. He gulped down the tea – a bit weak for his taste – but welcome nonetheless. He dressed quickly and was satisfied he looked smart and ready for duty. He wasn't sure what to do with his soiled collar and cuffs. They were inferior to the ones he'd been loaned, so he could hardly leave his behind in their place.

He decided to stuff them in his coat pocket and then have the borrowed ones laundered and returned, but how that was to be accomplished he had no notion.

The two of them strolled as casual as you like back to the racecourse as if nothing untoward had taken place the night before. Outwardly everywhere was calm but he noticed there were more uniformed peelers around today. Fortunately, none of them were known to him so his disguise was not revealed.

'Do we walk around to the stables or what?'

'I think as my secretary it would be in order for you to view the horses again. I shall go in search of his lordship. If he had been arrested we would have heard of it.'

Alfie preferred Ascot quiet like what it was now before the crush of racegoers arrived for the first race at midday. The gambling booths were quiet, the parade ring empty. As he walked past the grandstand he could see several of the rooms overlooking the track were busy.

He hoped Silver Star was still there and had not been taken away to wherever she would live in future. Even if she could no longer race she was a valuable broodmare and he was quite certain someone would bid for her. He was astonished to find not only the mare's stall empty but also the stallion's and three more adjacent to these.

A passing stable boy saw him peering in and stopped to explain. 'Lord Fonsby's horses have been withdrawn and they left this morning.' He looked around before continuing. 'Some buggers tried to poison the mare and they was caught red-handed. Folks are saying it were a inside job, which is why all them horses belonging to his lordship have gone.'

'Good heavens! The gentleman I work for is hoping to purchase Silver Star. He will be most disappointed.' Alfie hoped his diction didn't reveal his true status.

'Good job he didn't; the mare's racing days are done. 'Scuse me, governor, I better get on or I'll be for it.'

Alfie returned to hang about outside the grandstand and he didn't have long to wait before the inspector came out. 'Well, we can leave now, Nightingale. Fonsby has resigned his membership of the Jockey Club and has had his licence revoked. He'll not be able to own a racehorse again.'

'The poor buggers what tried to do his dirty work, they weren't common villains but toffs. What's going to happen to them?'

'They haven't got away with it completely. They too are banned from ever attending the racecourse again. Their names are blackened beyond redemption and they will no longer be accepted in the circles they used to frequent.'

'If it had been a cove like me they'd be before the magistrate and doing several years' hard labour. It's one law for the rich and another for the poor.' He regretted his words. He weren't no Chartist, but too late to take them back.

'True, young man, but there's little you or I can do about it. Shall we repair to the hostelry and have an early luncheon before returning to Scotland Yard? There are things we need to discuss and it would probably be sensible to do it away from prying ears.'

'I never say no to a blowout, sir, especially if I ain't paying.'

In perfect harmony they walked to the inn and instead of beer he had a pot of excellent coffee and felt like a real gent. He was beginning to like being treated different – amazing what a change a good suit of clothes made. In future he were going to make an effort with his speech, try and improve his lot. Not that a detective were anything special, but he wanted to be given the cases what involved the better-off folk, not them what was like him.

'Now, to business. I've been watching your progress, young man, and there's more to you than any of your fellow constables. Today was by way of an experiment on my part – I wished to see if you could carry off the pretence of being someone you are not.'

'Did I pass your test, sir?'

'With flying colours, Nightingale. You carry yourself well, nothing shifty about you. We'll work on your language together. Do you get the gist of what I'm suggesting?'

'I'm to go up in the world, mix with middling folk and better. I ain't – I'm not going to say no to that. It's what I were – was – thinking myself.'

'Good man, you're getting the hang of it already. You are intelligent, quick to learn and I believe you will be able to blend in anywhere. The chief constable is eager to have a small team of detectives who can work with the grand folk without offending their sensibilities. I have been designated to set this up. You are my first recruit and I shall have you made up to sergeant as soon as I can arrange it, and then you must work to become an inspector.'

'It's what I want to do, what I always intended when I joined up last year.'

'Excellent. I am to be promoted to chief inspector and I shall be on the lookout for other candidates within the small group of detectives we already have.'

'Am I to return to Leman Street or do I now report to you at Scotland Yard?'

'To me in future. You will have to return to your billet and collect your belongings. I shall make arrangements for you to have accommodation nearby.'

'There is something that you don't know about me, sir. I'm a married man with two boys. I came to London to make something of myself with my wife's blessing. I'm hoping that I will be entitled to married accommodation eventually so I can move them here to be with me.'

'Thank you for telling me. Is there anything else you wish to divulge?'

Alfie hesitated. He wanted to be honest but revealing that he had forged his testimonials would probably mean instant dismissal. On the other hand, if he didn't then there was always the possibility the information would come out later and it would be far harder to lose the life he now looked forward to.

'I wrote the testimonials myself, Inspector. I hadn't been in Chelmsford long enough to ask anyone to vouch for me.'

'I am relieved that you have told me, Nightingale, because I discovered that for myself when I decided you were the man for me. Don't look so shocked, young man – we all have a few skeletons in our cupboards. You might find this hard to believe but it was the fact that you could produce such excellent forgeries that convinced me you were the perfect choice. You have obviously received a good education and that is essential if you are to do the job successfully.'

'I won't let you down. I promise you'll not regret taking me on.'

'I would not have done so if I had any doubts about your abilities. You have the remainder of the day to collect your belongings and find your new accommodation.'

'There is one thing I haven't asked. What do I do with my two uniforms? Also, is there an allowance made for plain-clothes?'

'Return everything you were issued with to the quartermaster at Leman Street. There will be some recompense for clothing especially as there will be occasions when you must be dressed as you are today. You will need to purchase a second set of garments, two spare shirts plus several collars and cuffs. Your usual clothes will be sufficient for some of your work.'

'I shall miss Fred, the cove what I – the man that I work with. He's become a good friend over these past months.'

'The road you are setting out on, Nightingale, will mean giving up things that you consider important. Being a member of the criminal investigation department must be your priority in future.'

The inspector didn't say so, but it was obvious from his words that he included Betty and the boys in this warning. He weren't sure if any job were worth losing his family for. Nevertheless, he'd give it a go for a few months and then decide.

14

COLCHESTER, AUGUST 1849

The business continued to grow and Sarah had more than enough customers to make a good living and support her many dependents. Since Ada and her three youngest – Fred, Beth and Annie – had moved in last month the house had reached its capacity.

Ada's children were all at school so she took over the care of the little ones, which meant Betty was now in charge of the shop. Having this responsibility was exactly what her friend needed and she was proving an asset.

John did all of the deliveries and collections and proudly pushed his own smartly painted barrow around Colchester. The shop, of course, closed on Sunday and Sarah gave all her staff the day off. With Ada and Betty and herself, it was no problem to cook and clean for the ten of them for one day a week.

'Ma, why isn't John back yet?' Mary asked. Her brother had promised to take her and Tommy down to the river with Spot on his return.

'I don't know, love. I expect he's been asked to deliver something else for one of our customers. He'll be back soon enough. Why don't you wait in the garden and play with Jimmy? Auntie Ada is out there.'

Her daughter trotted off, her concern about her missing brother forgotten for the moment. Sarah hadn't realised John had been gone for more than two hours on an errand that should have taken half that time.

She went into the shop and beckoned Betty over. 'I'm going to look for John. Do you have the addresses he was delivering to?'

'I do. One was halfway down East Hill and the other in West Stockwell Street.'

Her stomach lurched. This was where Hatch had run his illegal business. If she had known John was going there she would have suggested he took the dog with him.

'I won't be long.' There was no need for her to tell her friend why she was going – from Betty's expression she understood the significance of the address.

'I'm sorry, I've been so busy I didn't think…'

'We've been back three months and had no trouble. When Davie came two weeks ago he said everything was quiet and trade had begun to pick up again at my mother's shop. Why would either of us consider it dangerous for John to go to Stockwell Street?'

The dog was playing with the children on the small patch of grass. She called his name and waved his rope and he bounded over. He never said no to a walk.

'Ada, I'm just going out and I thought I'd take Spot. The children must remain with you for the moment.'

She wanted to pick up her skirts and run but steadied her breathing and walked briskly instead, even stopping to greet the occasional customer politely when necessary. She turned right into Nunn's Cut Road, which would return her directly to the street she wanted.

This end of Colchester was not as poor as Barrack Street where she had lived for a short while, but she still stood out here in her smart green gown with matching bonnet. The dog pressed himself against her thigh and she felt his hackles rise and he began to growl softly.

Standing on the corner were three men. They weren't drunk, which was a blessing, but they were looking at her askance and this was enough to set the dog off. He was as gentle as a lamb with all the family but woe betide an outsider who threatened any of them.

'Hush now. Good boy, I don't want to annoy them.'

The dog's snarls became audible and the watchers hastily stepped into an archway, allowing her to walk past unmolested. Her heart was thudding uncomfortably. She was checking the numbers on the doors and arrived at the one her son had delivered to.

She knocked loudly on the door but received no response. An old lady who was scrubbing her step a few doors down sat back on her heels. 'There ain't no one living there, missus. They left a few weeks ago.'

Sarah hurried up to her. 'My son was delivering a gown for a Mrs Andrews at this address. There has obviously been some mistake. Did you see him come? It would have been an hour or so ago.'

'No, there ain't been no one knocking on the door apart from you today. Just you wait there, missus, I'll ask my Sam. He were out and about all morning and is bound to have seen him.'

For an old lady she was remarkably spry and pushed herself upright, dried her arms and hands on her apron, dropped her scrubbing brush into the pail and gestured with her head that Sarah follow down the narrow passageway to the backyard.

'Sam, this lady wants a word.'

An elderly man appeared at the gate. He was toothless, hairless, but otherwise in good fettle. Sarah explained and his jolly smile vanished.

'I saw your boy a while back. He was being dragged along by two nasty beggars and didn't look none too happy about it. There weren't no sign of his barrow.'

'Where did they take him?'

The old man looked around as if thinking he might be overheard. 'There's an old warehouse behind the house that Mr Hatch lived in. I reckon he's in there. You don't want to go anywhere near it, missus. You need to find a constable and take him with you.'

'Thank you for your concern, but my dog is better than a constable. I would be grateful if you could raise the alarm for me. I fear if I wait for assistance my son might be dead. Hatch holds a grudge against me even though he has now married my mother.'

* * *

London, August 1849

Alfie was concerned he couldn't say his farewells to his friend and had to leave him a note instead. It was unlikely they would cross paths again as they both worked seven days a week and would now move in a different direction.

His uniforms were handed in and he was given a chit to say he had done so. Then, with his battered carpetbag under one arm, he began the long trek through London to Westminster. He couldn't afford the luxury of a taxi – he was going to have to dip into his own money in order to find the necessary garments for his new role in the police force.

The lodgings he were directed to were a sight better than the dismal cottage he'd been sharing these past nine months. He had a room to himself. It were decently furnished, had its own fireplace and even a rug on the boards. There were a proper kitchen, scullery, and water what came directly into the house. None of them newfangled taps what turned on and off, but a pump handle were good enough for him. This room were unpleasantly warm as the range were burning.

The privy was a wonder to behold – one of them ones what flushed. No doubt the shit and such went direct into the Thames, which were why it stunk so bad in the summer. There was two other detectives sharing this cottage but they was absent when he arrived. There were a parlour – he'd gone up in the world and no mistake. His mouth curved at the thought of what the married quarters might be like if this was how the bachelors were housed.

He found his paper and were reading it when he heard the clatter of clogs in the alleyway outside. The next thing the back door opened. When he went to investigate and found a cheerful lady of middle years tying a spotlessly clean apron around her ample frame.

'You must be the new detective; I were told you were coming yesterday.'

This pleased Alfie as he hadn't actually been offered the job then. The inspector must have made his decision before the completion of the Ascot job. 'Pleased to meet you. Alfie Nightingale.'

She grinned. 'Maisie Smith, at your service. I comes in every day first thing and gets the breakfast for you, does the laundry and cleaning and then I comes back this time to get a hot meal ready. Your share of me wages is five bob a week.' He nodded meekly. 'I does the shopping too. I ain't stupid – I know you don't earn much. I get the cheapest cuts.'

He could hardly refuse as if he did so it would make him unpopular with the other men. But it were a hefty slice of his wages each week. Then his panic subsided. As a detective, he would be getting an extra ten bob a week towards his living and his clothing. More than enough to have the luxury of being looked after.

'When do you want your money? How do we settle up with you for the food and such?'

'Leave your share on the dresser of a Saturday, Alfie. I'll tell you what I'm owed on top of me wages.'

'It's Saturday today...'

'Bless you, you ain't to pay in advance. There's plenty here to feed you as well and I'm sure Bill and Mike won't mind you sharing this once.'

'That's grand. What time do we eat?'

'I have it ready for seven o'clock sharp. If the other lads can get back, then they do. If not, they can reheat it when they return. You'll have it nice and fresh today. It's mutton chops, taters and cabbage. There's always cake or something in the tin in the pantry.'

Alfie devoured his meal with relish. Maisie had dished his up and then left him to it. Neither Bill nor Mike appeared – they must be out on a job. He couldn't wait to get started in his new career. A lot of folk thought it wrong for detectives to set out to trap criminals by watching them before they committed the crime – but it were a new way and one what he approved of. They were also used to look into things after the event, but the inspector had told him there were so few of them, it were only the murder cases what they took on.

He took his plate and crockery into the scullery, washed them and left them to drain. Then he made himself a pot of tea and took a generous slice of the plum cake in the tin. This was the life, and no mistake. He were dressed in his usual clothes, smart enough but not like a gent as he'd been before.

It had just got dark when his peace was disturbed by a thunderous knocking on the front door. When he opened it he were faced by a uniformed constable.

'Who are you? I need a detective.'

'I'm a detective – Nightingale, I've just transferred from Leman Street. How can I help?'

'There's been a shooting at a public house. There's already a uniformed constable shot. My sergeant says he ain't sending another in to be killed and he needs someone in plain clothes to nab the murderer.'

'I'll get me shooter. You can tell me everything I need to know on the way.'

He pulled on his black coat and grabbed his top hat. It weren't much protection from a bullet, but might protect his head from a cosh. As they ran towards the premises the constable explained what had happened.

'The landlord takes in lodgers and one of them is as mad as a hatter. He shot an old lady and when a constable went in to apprehend him he put a bullet in his shoulder. He ain't dead, but he's badly hurt.'

'I don't see the urgency. Surely he can be taken easily enough by armed peelers?'

'He's got a hostage, the landlord's wife. He's threatening to kill her if anyone goes near him.'

They arrived at the public house to find it surrounded by interested spectators as well as half a dozen uniformed policemen. His arrival was greeted with enthusiasm. A tall, thin man with the stripes of a sergeant shook his hand.

'He's there, in that chamber on the corner. Do you have your gun with you?'

'Loaded and ready, sir. I don't see how I'm to do what you cannot just because I'm not in a uniform, but I'll do my best.'

'It was a good move, Nightingale, to come like a gent. He won't suspect you're the law.'

Alfie couldn't for the life of him see how that were going to help. 'What's the man's name?'

'John Dodd. The landlord's wife is Sue Blunt.'

He thought this a fool's errand, but he'd no option but to try and rescue Mrs Blunt and take the mad shooter into custody.

* * *

Colchester, August 1849

Sarah was about to head for the warehouse when she remembered that Mr Daniel, who had bought Alfie's cottage and business, lived only a few minutes away. He too had one of Buster's sons – two dogs would be better than one.

Regardless of the startled stares she got from those she ran past she continued in a headlong rush until she reached the front door. She hammered on it hoping he might be in, although at this time of the day it was unlikely.

The door opened and he took one look at her and nodded, his face grim. 'I'll be a minute, Mrs Cooper. I'll just get my coat and things.'

She didn't need to ask what things he was referring to. He would be bringing a weapon of some sort. She must have been mad to even consider going down to find John on her own. This was Hatch's work. She should have known he wouldn't allow her to live unmolested in Colchester – not whilst he had not had his revenge on Alfie.

Mr Daniel slammed the door shut and locked it. His dog looked more like Buster than Spot did. He was three inches taller and the same brownish grey. The two dogs sniffed each other's private parts and walked stiff-legged around each other for a few moments and then tails were wagging and they were the best of friends.

'What's happened? Tell me as we go.'

His expression became fierce when he had heard her story. 'I should never have let him go out on his own. This is all my fault.'

'No, it isn't. If anyone's to blame, it's me. I heard talk that Hatch knew how successful your business is and was determined to ruin it for you. I should have come around and warned you.'

'The warehouse is just round the corner.'

'You stop here, Mrs Cooper. I'll take the two dogs. This is no task for a lady.'

There was no point in arguing as he strode ahead and unless she ran she couldn't keep up with him. She allowed him to turn the corner and then raced after him. Nothing, not even danger to herself, would keep her from her son.

The first thing she saw was the smart new barrow smashed into pieces. The warehouse was open and she was still a few yards from it when the dogs attacked. A man screamed. She burst through the door to see Mr Daniel cracking a man across the head with his cosh. Spot was at the throat of one man who was ominously silent and the other dog was tearing lumps from a third man. It was his screams she had heard.

Ignoring the mayhem and gore she looked around frantically for her son. Her heart almost stopped when she saw a crumpled blood-covered shape in the corner. With a moan she dropped to his side and felt frantically for a pulse. Thank God! He was still alive, but barely. How could anyone have beaten a child so badly? The men deserved to die for their filthy actions.

'Don't try and move him, love. I'll fetch a cart and we'll take him home on that. The racket had attracted the attention of a few urchins who were gawping in the door, their eyes wide, faces pale, as they viewed the carnage.

'Run and fetch the doctor. Ask him to come here immediately. I shall give you a sixpence.' She was surprised her voice was so normal-sounding when inside she was panicking.

The two dogs were still snarling and the one conscious man was whimpering but not saying anything coherent. 'John, darling boy, Ma is here. We'll soon have you home and make you well again.'

The boy didn't stir. She was certain one leg was broken and one arm. He also had a head injury. It was this that gave her the most concern. She pulled up her skirt and ripped off a large chunk of her petticoat. This was torn into strips and she folded one into a pad and placed it on the wound on the side of his head and then tied another strip around to hold it in place.

He was too cold, his skin clammy and a strange bluish colour. How could this have happened? Why had she thought it safe to come back to Colchester? She should have taken the family to Romford or even to London and not risked her precious children by returning here.

In the distance she heard the trundle of wooden wheels on the cobbles

– good, Mr Daniel was coming back with the transport. Then, added to this was the distinct noise of a man running in their direction. She prayed it was the doctor. When he had taken care of Alfie after Hatch had had him beaten almost to death, she had been impressed with him.

'By God, has it come to this? How could anyone treat a child like this?' The physician dropped to his knees beside her and she moved aside so he could see the damage.

He ran his hand up and down the limbs, muttering and cursing under his breath at what he found. 'Your son has both a broken leg and arm. He could well have sustained some broken ribs as well. His spine appears undamaged. It is the head wound and the fact that he is so deeply unconscious that worries me, Mrs Cooper.'

'He is so cold and still. He must have lost a lot of blood from his head wound.'

'I shall put a temporary splint on his limbs and then we can wrap him in this warm flannel and blanket. He should really go to the hospital...'

'No, I shall nurse him at home. He will do better in familiar surroundings when he does waken.'

Mr Daniel pushed a barrow alongside and he and the doctor gripped the sides of the blanket and gently lifted him onto it.

The child who had fetched the doctor waited hopefully by the door for his reward. Only then she realised she hadn't brought her purse with her.

'Here, for your troubles. Now you run ahead to number sixty North Hill and tell them we're coming.' Mr Daniel tossed the boy a coin and then grasped the handles of the barrow and wheeled it forward. Being bounced and bumped over the cobbles was not going to improve John's condition.

'Wait – I think it would be better for him if you carried him. Do it the same way you just lifted him from the ground,' Sarah said.

The doctor nodded. 'Yes, I should have thought of that myself.'

Together the two men lifted John and so began the slow walk back. Folk gathered as they passed and she heard the tutting and muttering and many called out in sympathy. When they eventually arrived home, Betty was waiting on the pavement, her face ashen and tear-streaked.

'The monsters, to do this to an innocent child. It doesn't bear thinking of.'

'The dogs killed one of them and maimed another – I think Mr Daniel disposed of the third. We shall have to inform the constables.'

Mr Daniel answered, his voice gruff. 'I'll deal with all that, Mrs Cooper. Hatch went too far this time. Did you hear what was being said? His men won't be popular around this neighbourhood any longer.'

'May he and his minions rot in hell for what they did to my boy.'

15

The two men carried her darling boy up to his bedroom. Ada had already prepared the room. The curtains were drawn, the bedcovers folded back, and a temporary bed set up alongside so Sarah could sleep beside him until he was recovered.

Mr Daniel nodded and left the doctor to do his work. Betty appeared with hot water, clean cloths and neatly rolled bandages made from soft linen offcuts from the workshop.

'You stop here, Sarah; I'll take care of the children and everything else. I'll bring your meals on a tray so you don't have to leave him.'

She noticed then there was a commode placed discreetly behind a battered lacquered screen in the far corner of the room. The chest of drawers usually served as a nightstand. Now the china basin and jug had been moved to a small table, which had been brought in for the purpose, leaving the surface clear for anything that might be needed to nurse the patient.

Doctor Adams worked quietly and efficiently. As he straightened limbs and applied splints and bandages, he talked softly to the comatose child. At no time did John make a murmur. This terrified her as setting his broken arm and leg must have been hideously painful.

It took an hour for him to complete his work. He tipped water into the basin and washed his hands thoroughly before drying them on the towel.

'I'm sanguine that your son's leg will be as good as new, also his arm, as long as he remains in bed for three weeks. After that he can be carried downstairs and put on a daybed.'

'Thank you, Doctor Adams, I'm glad he will not be lame. Why has he not recovered consciousness?'

'I'm afraid, Mrs Cooper, that the head injury might prove to be fatal. Seldom does a patient recover when they are so deeply unconscious. We know little about the brain and I can only speculate. You must try and get liquid into him as often as possible.'

'Will it harm him to have visitors? Does he need to be kept in the dark and in silence?'

'I think keeping the curtains drawn is a good idea. I would say no children in here for the moment. However, you can talk to him, read him stories even if he appears to be unaware. Hearing your voice might bring him back to you. One can but hope.'

'Then I shall do that. I shall remain with him constantly.' She dropped onto the bed that had been brought in for her. 'How long can he remain like this before he dies?'

'I have known patients to remain in a coma for weeks but this has been following an apoplexy not a head injury. I'm sorry to say that if your son does not recover consciousness in the next few days, I fear he will never do so. You must prepare yourself for the worst.'

'I must send word to my middle son who lives in Chelmsford. I'm sure his master will allow him to visit as the matter is so urgent.'

'Don't hesitate to call me again if his condition worsens. I shall give my statement at the police station. I can assure you there will be no repercussions from the deaths of those vile men.'

He had now got all his instruments back in his leather bag and was ready to depart. Wearily she pushed herself up. 'That is one thing I don't have to worry about. Could you ask Mrs Nightingale to come up on your way out?'

'Of course I will. You cannot nurse day and night without a break, Mrs

Cooper. However hard it might be, you must allow your friends to take their turn unless you too wish to be under my care.'

* * *

London, August 1849

When Alfie and the constable arrived at the public house, there were already a dozen or more people standing about waiting to see what would happen. The two constables were doing their best to keep the drunken rabble in order. A hostage taken and the possible shooting of a detective weren't something what happened every day.

Once they were inside Alfie asked the layout of the upstairs. 'What's this fellow agitated about? Does he have a violent nature?'

The landlord was wringing his hands, his fat, red face tear-streaked. He might cheat his customers, water his beer, but he obviously loved his wife.

'He's always been a bit odd. Given to outbursts for no reason, but he ain't ever been violent to no one. No idea what's set him off today. Didn't know he owned a shooter neither.'

'Right then. I'm armed, but I hope it won't come to that.' Alfie checked his shooter was ready to fire and easy to access and then made his way to the upstairs as silently as he could. He paused on the landing. The door he wanted was at the far end of the narrow passageway – he would have known without instructions as he could hear movement.

He pressed himself against the wall so if the man fired through the door he wouldn't be the target. The second door he had to edge past was open but he didn't think anything of it. Then this flew open and he were confronted by the madman. He had no time to get out his own weapon. He were staring imminent death in the face.

'Put your gun down. You do not wish to shoot a policeman.'

'I'll teach you to interfere with me, peeler or not.'

He stared into the man's distorted face. There were no reasoning with him. If by some miracle he wasn't killed he would go straight down to

Chelmsford and be reunited with his family. He'd give up his new career if Betty and the boys didn't want to come and live with him in the Smoke.

The muzzle of the gun pressed into his forehead. The madman pulled the trigger. His knees almost buckled as the gun didn't fire. Before his assailant could reload, his own pistol was out. He reversed it and knocked the man unconscious.

He turned him over with his boot and quickly handcuffed him. His hands were shaking. He couldn't believe he was still alive. He picked the gun up. *Bugger!* Why hadn't the gun fired? Alfie strode to the villain's bedchamber and pushed open the door.

The wife of the landlord was trussed up like a Christmas fowl. He untied her. She didn't stop to thank him but ran off sobbing noisily, leaving him to examine the room. He saw at once what had happened. On a shelf was two tins side by side, one containing gunpowder the other containing tea. The man had charged the gun with shot and tea instead of shot and powder.

He was smiling when he came out of the room. The two constables was astounded by his story.

'This will be the talk of the station, Mr Nightingale. I reckon you're the luckiest man alive,' one of them said as he clapped him on the back.

'I'll leave you to take the bastard to the station. I've got some business to attend to.'

He returned to his billet, grabbed his wallet and shoved all his belongings into his battered carpetbag. He were lucky to be alive. He weren't wasting another minute. He were going to catch the next train to Chelmsford. He would write resigning his position before he set off, then post it if Betty took him back.

* * *

Liverpool Street Station was full of smoke, steam and soot. The racket from the clanking engines drowned out the yelling and such from the guards and passengers. He purchased his ticket and headed for the platform. He were in luck. There were a train about to leave for Colchester.

Carriages was now supposed to be enclosed, even third class, but not all trains had been altered. He selected an empty compartment in second class and hoped no one would join him. As the smoke and smells of London were left behind to be replaced by green fields and trees, he knew he had made the right decision. He weren't going back – he had his few belongings in his carpetbag.

He had written his letter of resignation and addressed it to the inspector but had yet to post it. He would do so when he arrived in Chelmsford. His place was with his family regardless of the circumstances. He would deal with that bastard Hatch and make sure he didn't harm them. He were lucky to be alive and he wasn't going to waste another minute of his life living apart from them.

The train chugged into Chelmsford and he disembarked, eager to get around to the shop and surprise Betty and Sarah. He had got as far as the forecourt when he remembered the young man what had warned him not to go to his house. Perhaps it would be wise to speak to him before he went there, to know the lay of the land.

It took him a few minutes to locate the guard he wanted. The young man recognised him immediately, despite him being dressed like a toff.

'Mr Nightingale, ain't you a sight for sore eyes. No point in you going to find your missus – she ain't there any longer. They moved to Colchester a few months back. Your ma married Mr Hatch and he lives there now.'

'Have they all moved?'

'Apart from Davie. He's apprenticed to a cabinetmaker. It ain't far from here. You've got plenty of time before the next train to visit.'

'I'll do that. He can tell me what's what before I go to Colchester.'

He thought of Davie as his nephew, as he did the other two boys, and he would be pleased to catch up with him. Joe must be back from his travels by now as well. It had been far too long since he'd spoken to any of his family and it were all his own fault.

He found the workshop and walked in. There were a decent-sized showroom displaying examples of what were made here. He were most impressed by the miniatures. The baby chair and crib were taken from his own design, so might well have been made by Davie.

The bell on the door had rung as he entered and he didn't have long to wait before a neatly dressed woman bustled in.

'Good morning, sir, how can I be of assistance?'

'Morning. I'm Davie's uncle. Could he be spared from his work for a minute to speak to me? I ain't seen him for over a year.'

Her pleasant expression turned to sadness. 'I'm very sorry, Mr Nightingale, but Davie's not here at the moment. His younger brother, John, has suffered a dreadful accident and he was called to be by his bedside yesterday.'

'I'm on my way to Colchester – thank God I decided to come today.' He didn't stop to ask what sort of accident. All that mattered to him was that the little lad must be at death's door for Davie to be summoned. He turned to go and then realised he didn't know whereabouts his family was living. 'Can you give me the address?'

'I can indeed. Number sixty North Hill. I pray you are in time.'

Alfie swallowed the lump in his throat. 'Do you know if Davie's older brother Joe is there?'

'No, Davie told us the ship that he and Mr Billings sailed on has been lost at sea.'

He blundered out into the sunshine, his eyes blurred, unable to respond to this second blow. He'd arrived here with high spirits and now everything had changed. Sarah would be beside herself. First Dan killed, and then Robert and Joe lost at sea. He weren't a praying man, didn't think much of a God who let folk die so easily, but as he trudged back to the station he asked the Almighty to let John live.

* * *

Colchester, August 1849

There was no change in John's condition – but at least he wasn't getting any worse. Sarah spooned some boiled water between his dry lips for the umpteenth time that evening. A tray had been sent up to her but it was untouched, apart from the tea, which she had drunk.

Word had been sent to Davie and she expected him to arrive at any moment. He was already devastated by the apparent loss of his older brother and now it seemed very likely was going to lose his younger brother too. She read to John from his favourite book, one full of adventurous tales in far-off places.

The door had been left ajar but strangely she had heard nothing from the little ones or anyone else in the house. They must be creeping about on tiptoes. How was she going to explain the situation to Mary? Tears trickled down her cheeks unheeded and she tried to pray but found it difficult. If there was a God, he certainly paid no attention to the likes of them.

With the curtains drawn it was impossible to know what the time was. A single candle flickered on the mantelshelf, just enough to see by but not enough to disturb the patient. Were the children in bed? She dribbled a little more water into his mouth and then went to the door. She needed to relieve herself so would find out what the rest of the house was doing at the same time. John hadn't changed over the past few hours and she doubted he would do so in the few minutes she would be gone.

She collected the candle and stepped into the corridor, shocked to find it inky black and all the bedchamber doors firmly closed. It must be far later than she had thought. There was a clock in the kitchen – she would check the time whilst she was downstairs, but first she must use the WC.

Everyone was asleep. Another cup of tea would be nice – she would stir up the range and put the kettle on to boil. The time was a little after two in the morning; small wonder it was so quiet. As she filled the kettle she heard footsteps outside and then someone rattled the gate.

Davie had come. He must have caught the mail train. When she let him in he flung his arms around her and she embraced him. 'Am I too late, Ma? Has he gone?'

'No, son, he is still with us, but only just. Leave your boots by the door. You'll have to walk about in your socks. Make the tea and cut yourself a slice of cake if you want it. Bring it up when it's ready. Don't forget to bank down the range.'

She hurried back, not wishing to be away from John a moment longer. From the light of the candle she could see no change in him. He was breathing, but only just. His colour was bad, pallid, and he'd not stirred at all since the doctor had set his limbs. There was laudanum on the chest of drawers for when he came round. The doctor had said he would need it for the pain.

The door to Betty's room opened and her friend came out in her nightclothes. 'Any change? I thought I heard Davie arrive. Is there anything I can do?'

'No, I want to stay with him tonight. Now Davie's here I might risk a nap on the bed. Were the children very distressed?'

'They were upset, but stoic. Spot was beside himself and I had to shut him in the scullery as he was making so much racket.'

'Maybe having his dog beside him might help him wake. I'll ask the doctor when he calls.'

For the remainder of the night they took it in turns to sit beside John. The early morning sunshine filtered through the drawn curtains and she blew out the candle. Davie was stretched out on the bed fast asleep. He had said he wasn't going back to Chelmsford whatever happened.

He was indentured, was legally obliged to remain with his master until he completed his apprenticeship. His employer, from what little she knew about him, seemed a reasonable man. Perhaps he would release Davie from his contract if she offered him some money. He had refused payment for the apprenticeship although he was entitled to it.

Either way, she was glad her son had decided to stay in Colchester. If John didn't breathe his last in the next few days then his recovery was going to be long and painful. Having his brother here would make it so much easier for the lad.

The church clock had struck four a while ago. Another hour before anyone would be up. She was desperately tired and decided to stretch out beside the sleeping form on the bed. There was no danger she wouldn't hear the patient if he stirred. A mother, even when asleep, was aware of the needs of her children.

She was woken from a fitful slumber when Davie spoke to her. 'Ma, I'm going to take Spot for a walk. I won't be long. No change but he ain't no worse.'

Groggily she sat up and rubbed her eyes, which felt as if they were full of grit. 'Have I been asleep long?'

'Not sure. It's six now. I heard someone go down to the kitchen. I'll ask the girl to bring you up some tea and toast.'

She rolled out of bed and padded over to John. His colour seemed a little better now, not quite so pale, and his lips were not as blue.

'Good morning, darling boy. I'm going to give you some more water.' She managed to get three spoonfuls down him but he was worryingly still. The physician would be visiting later that morning and hopefully would give a better prognosis than he had been able to offer yesterday.

Her gown was sadly creased. It looked as if she'd slept in it – which she had. When Davie got back she would get her daughter up herself and change into fresh garments.

The morning seemed interminable and when the doctor had come he had not been hopeful about the outcome. 'The longer your son is unconscious, Mrs Cooper, the less chance there is of him recovering.'

'Davie wants to bring the dog upstairs – will this do any harm?'

'Do whatever you think will rouse the boy. I shall call tomorrow but don't hesitate to send for me if his condition changes.'

Ada had taken the children to the castle where there was to be some sort of entertainment. It would be better if they were out of the house at the moment.

Davie arrived at the bedchamber door with Spot beside him. He was holding tight to his collar in case the animal tried to jump on the bed.

'Shall I bring him in, Ma?'

'Yes, but make sure he doesn't disturb John.'

'I thought that was the idea.'

The dog somehow sensed he had to be quiet and made no attempt to leap about the place as he was wont to do when allowed inside. Instead he sat down next to the bed and put his huge head on the pillow beside John and gently nudged him. When he got no response, he whined softly and then licked his face.

To her astonishment and delight John's eyes flickered open. She was at his side in a second.

'Sweetheart, welcome back. Don't try and move – you have a broken leg and arm and they must remain still.'

His gaze turned to her. Her stomach clenched. He was looking at her with no recognition. In fact, she wasn't even sure he could see.

'Davie's come to live with us again.'

'You don't look too clever, John, but I'll soon have you on your feet and running around again – don't you fret about that.'

Again, the little boy's expression remained blank. Then the dog nudged him a second time and he smiled.

'Good dog, you stay here with John. Don't climb on the bed.' Spot's tail thumped the floor as if he understood every word she'd said. Sarah moved away and drew Davie with her.

'Do you think he's blind or just doesn't recognise us?'

'It don't make no never mind, Ma. He's conscious and wants the dog with him.'

'I'm going to send word to Doctor Adams. He will want to see for himself that John is awake.'

16

Alfie completed the walk to North Hill fast. It were almost dark and he didn't want to arrive when the house was locked for the night. He found the shop easy enough and was stunned to see his own name above the door. The blinds were drawn but there were a light shining from what must be the front parlour.

The front door was the one to the shop but if he knocked on the window whoever was in there would look out and see him on the pavement. The curtain twitched and then was pulled right back and Betty was staring at him as if he were an apparition.

Bugger! He should have taken off his topper – it were likely she didn't properly recognise him. Hastily he removed it and he heard her squeal of delight.

'Go round the side, Alfie. I'll let you in.'

He hadn't noticed the archway or he'd have gone there first. His heart was thudding something painful. From her face he thought John weren't dead, must still be alive at least. Then the gate swung open and she was in his arms.

He held her close and when she looked up he kissed her fiercely. 'Betty love, can you forgive me? I ain't going nowhere ever again if you'll have me back.'

'Don't be daft. I've missed you every minute. How did you know that John was so poorly? That's why you've come, isn't it?'

'He's still alive then. I feared I were going to be too late. How is he?'

She pulled him in and bolted the gate behind them. 'He's awake, but... but, the doctor thinks he might have lost his wits and he's blind too.'

'He were at death's door yesterday, love, so still being with us is something to be thankful for.'

The back door was open but the house was quiet. 'My boys? Are they well? Can I see them?'

Her smile was blinding. 'Tomorrow, Alfie, no point in waking them now. Leave your boots there with the others.'

He noticed the row of outdoor shoes and bent down to unlace his own footwear. He couldn't see much of the premises but what he could see impressed him.

'Come into the front parlour. I'm taking over from Sarah in the sickroom at ten o'clock so we've got plenty of time to talk. I'll get the kettle on, shall I?'

'That would be grand. If there's a bit of bread and cheese going I'd be that grateful. I ain't eaten since last night.'

She directed him through the house and then rushed off to the kitchen. He had forgotten how pretty his wife was, how her eyes sparkled and her fair hair shone in the candlelight. He were a lucky man to have her take him back. From now on he would be the best husband and father he could, and do whatever he was asked to without complaint.

He tossed his hat onto a chair and shrugged off his jacket. As he did so something heavy bumped against his arm and he remembered he still had the shooter the inspector had given him. He would have to return it in person. When things were better here, he'd take Betty and the boys with him, show them off like; he were that proud to have such a family. Whilst they were there he could withdraw his savings from the bank and bring it back with him.

The room looked familiar somehow. His mouth curved. This were his own furniture. Daniel had given it back to Betty. Then the door flew open and Sarah hurtled into his arms.

'I can't tell you how happy I am to have you home. Betty will be beside herself with happiness. She's prayed every day that you would come back to her and the boys. I can't believe you've turned up just when we most need you.'

'It were a coincidence. Something happened to me what made me think. I went to see Davie and his master told me about John. Were he trampled by a horse?'

'No, Hatch's men were responsible. I should never have brought us here. We should have gone somewhere else to start again.'

For a second, he was blinded by a rage so fierce his head spun. 'I'll make sure he don't harm no one else.'

'No, there has been enough violence. Sit down and I'll tell you how we all come to be here.'

'You need to be with the lad; it can wait until tomorrow. I've got plenty to tell you, might as well do it in one go.'

'You're right. I must go up. By the by, Ada and her three youngest live here too.' She kissed him on the cheek and rushed out.

Betty returned with his supper and whilst he devoured it he regaled her with his life for the past year.

'Well I never did! Alfie Nightingale a policeman? I'll move to London with you, love. You don't have to give up your promotion to be with us.'

* * *

The dog woke her up by pushing his cold, wet nose into her face. She was out of bed before she was properly awake but John was still sound asleep.

'Do you want to go out? Come along, I'll let you into the garden.'

She opened the door but instead of rushing downstairs he bounded to Betty and Alfie's room, scratched at it and whined.

'Hush, you'll wake everyone up.'

Alfie spoke from behind the door. 'Give us a minute. I'll be out and can take you for a walk.'

The dog sat in front of the door, his long tail swishing back and forth like a broom. Her brother emerged, his hair tousled. He turned as he left. 'You sleep in, love. I'll see to the boys when they wake.' He closed the door quietly and his expression told her everything she needed to know.

'Look in on John before you go down. The children don't get up until seven, which gives you an hour or more for your walk.'

He stood beside her looking down at his nephew. 'If them bastards wasn't dead already, I'd finish them off. To do this to a child – it don't bear thinking of.'

'Doctor Adams said that his arm and leg will heal. He is hopeful his sight will return too, even if his mind remains damaged. He can still have a happy life. He won't remember how he was, so we mustn't be sad for him.'

Alfie leant down and kissed the sleeping child. He murmured something but she couldn't catch the words. She had time to have a thorough wash this morning and put on one of her new gowns in honour of the occasion. Ada had a box room to herself, barely room for a single bed, but better than being obliged to share with her children.

She tapped on the door and got an immediate response. Everyone had been on edge expecting to get the worst possible news. Ada was overjoyed to hear John was better and that her brother had come back.

'Good things go in threes, Sarah love – you see if I'm not right. Our sons will come home too.'

'I pray that you're correct. I have fallen behind with my cutting. Could I ask you to look in on John? I shall be in the workroom until breakfast.'

She had cut three gowns when something occurred to her. She frowned and put down her scissors. There was an empty building at the end of the garden that might be perfect for Davie and Alfie to set up a carpentry shop. Her son could do the fine work; Alfie could teach him what he needed to know. Her feet were wet from the dew – she should have stopped to put on her clogs and not ventured down the garden in her indoor shoes.

The door was stuck. Her attempts to pull it open failed and she was about to return when Spot arrived at her side, her brother close behind him.

When she told him why she was out here his smile said it all. 'Davie ain't going back then? Won't the law be after him?'

'I don't think so. He's determined to stay here and has already offered to make me another barrow. I thought we could employ Mr Daniel for all our deliveries and collections and you and Davie can concentrate on making tables, dressers and maybe some of the miniature cribs and chairs for the wealthy to buy for their children.'

'I reckon that could work a treat. I'd better get in. I told Betty I'd see to the children.'

'Alfie, you haven't seen them for a year. Jimmy won't remember you and Tommy might well be shy.'

'I ain't bothered about that as long as I'm here now. They'll soon forget I left them.'

The house was awake. Sally was busy knocking back the dough that had been rising at the back of the range all night. Everybody ate breakfast and lunch in the kitchen; only the evening meal was served more formally in the dining room.

'I'd better warn you the house is somewhat crowded, Alfie. There are five girls living in. Sally is our cook as she was in Chelmsford; the others take it in turns to do housework and work in the shop. Betty is in charge of that now. Ada looks after the children. We have two women who come in to do the laundry and heavy work.'

His laugh was loud in the early morning garden. 'Bloody hell! This family has gone up in the world. Who'd have thought it? Where are you intending to squeeze in Robert and Joe when they get back?'

She blushed and he laughed again. 'You know very well that Robert and I will be getting married. Joe will have to share with John and Davie. I'm hoping that once he's able to get out of bed things will be less difficult.'

'I don't reckon Robert will want to live here. He'll buy you a nice house of your own.'

'You're right. We intended to find a house in Lexden large enough to accommodate all of us, but I don't think I will want to move out so far. Perhaps we will be able to find something that will suit close by. Betty and I have discussed this at length. This house will be yours.'

'I reckon you can take the cook and the maids with you. Not sure I'm comfortable being waited on hand and foot.'

'I think you'd better discuss this with your wife, Alfie. Things are different for all of us. We've all changed over the past year and you need to understand that if you want to be happy here.'

'I ain't bothered who lives where or does what as long as I've got me family. I weren't sure if Betty would take me back. I told her everything last night and she told me what was what with you. That bastard has a lot to answer for.'

'I still don't know what you were doing this past year.'

'I were a peeler first and then promoted to detective. I need to go to speak to the inspector. If John's out of danger I'll go today. I were going to take Betty and the boys but she ain't keen to go yet.'

'A policeman? I can scarcely believe my ears. Are you quite sure you want to give it up and go back to being a carpenter?'

He didn't answer immediately and this worried her. She touched his arm. 'Betty says she'd be happy to move to the Smoke. She were that tickled I were doing so well and likely to get a promotion.'

'The decision is yours then. Return to a promising career and work seven days a week for little money or remain here and build up your own business and have time to spend with your family.'

'Put it like that and it makes me choice easy. I'm going nowhere. Me place is here. Betty will have to tell you why I came back so sudden. I've got to get in and get me boys up.'

'I'll come with you and get Mary. She shares the room with your boys. We won't wake them – better to let children sleep if you can.'

* * *

Alfie followed up the stairs and waited for his sister to open the door. It were like a blow to the chest seeing his sons sleeping. He padded to Jimmy's bed and stood looking down at him. He scarcely recognised the sleeping form. He'd been away too long – that was for sure.

Tommy weren't that different – older like – but still the same little lad he remembered. It were babies what changed so quickly. He moved across to look at his niece. She were the image of Sarah and no mistake. He backed away and didn't speak until the door was closed softly behind them.

'Little angels, all clean and pink, breaks me heart when I think of the kids around Whitechapel. It ain't right that we've got so much and they ain't got nothing at all.'

Sarah hugged him. 'It's how things are. We've both lived like that in the past and it just makes me more determined to make sure my family stays safe.' Spot slunk past them and nudged John's door open. 'I'm just going to check he's still asleep.'

Seeing John all bandaged and bruised just made him more determined to make those responsible pay with their lives. Another reason why he weren't going to stay a policeman. Prisoners was roughed up regularly in the cells but murder were another thing. It would be justice but the law wouldn't see it like that.

'I'm going to speak to Betty. I need to go to Scotland Yard sharpish. I'll be back before dark.'

His wife stirred as he came in and then pushed herself up on the bed. Her hair was loose around her shoulders, and her eyes sparkled. She were still as pretty as the first time he'd seen her. He kissed her and then quickly told her about the shooter.

'You will come back, won't you? The boys will be that excited when I tell them their pa's coming home for good.'

'I ain't staying away from you again. I got to go to the bank and get me money out as well as speak to the inspector. He'll try and persuade me to stay – but I ain't going to, never you worry.'

'Aren't you going to put on your smart togs? You look a real gent with your top hat and all.'

'No, I'm an ordinary cove. I'll stick to me normal things.'

'I got together a new set of clothes for you, hoping you'd come back. You'll find them in the closet over there.'

'Ta, that's grand. Never expected you to think of me like that. If I get off now; I'll get the early train.'

As he was passing the kitchen Sally handed him a small, brown paper parcel. 'Here, you'll need something to eat. It's well wrapped so you can have it on the train.'

'That's grand, just what I needed.'

* * *

He went to the bank and withdrew his money in flimsies. He dodged into an alley, removed a boot, and pushed the notes into his sock. No bugger would find them there even if he were done over.

Scotland Yard was busy. If he were still a detective he would be in trouble for reporting so late. He took the letter he'd written yesterday and approached the sergeant at the desk. He put the envelope down and then the shooter on top of it.

'Can you make sure this gets to Inspector Burgess?'

Alfie didn't wait around for a reply but scarpered sharpish. He didn't want to be asked to reconsider. He was letting the inspector down, but family came first.

He got off at Chelmsford and called in at the cabinetmaker's to update Davie's master. He didn't tell them his nephew weren't coming back – time enough for that when the dust settled. They was happy for the lad to stay away as long as necessary.

Ma's shop looked the same. It were busy enough, which were a good thing as when she were a widow she could keep herself and not come banging on their door asking for assistance. The bell attached to the door tinkled loudly and woman came in. 'How can I help you, sir? Are you looking for a gift for your wife?'

He stepped around her and into the house.

'No, no, you cannot go in there. You must come out at once or I shall call the constables.'

Ignoring her squawks, he closed the communicating door and bolted it. Next, he checked the reception rooms. His quarry weren't there, but he could hear voices in the office at the other end of the passageway. He unlatched the front door, leaving it slightly ajar – he might have to make a swift exit. With his back to the door he squared his shoulders and took a deep breath.

'Hatch, you bastard, get out here. I want to speak to you.'

A chair crashed to the floor and the door flew open. It weren't Hatch but his ma what stood there looking terrified.

'Alfie, what are you doing here? Come into the office. Don't shout – someone will fetch him.'

Then he noticed she had a split lip and a yellowing bruise on her cheek. She might have betrayed the family by marrying him, but he weren't leaving her here to be beaten up.

'Pack a bag, Ma – you're coming with me.'

The look of relief on her face were almost comical. She was out of the room like a rat from a drainpipe and back in five minutes. Her bonnet were on any old how, the carpetbag bulging, but she were smiling. He didn't reckon she done much of that lately.

This wasn't what he'd come for, but it were enough for now. He grabbed her elbow and pulled her out onto the pavement. 'There's a train in half an hour. We can talk then.'

The cove what was friendly with Davie took one look and scowled. 'In here, missus. I'll not let anyone find you. You too, Mr Nightingale. Better not to have fisticuffs on the station platform.'

'Thank you, I ain't going to forget your kindness.'

Once the door was firmly closed his breathing steadied. The last person Sarah wanted to see was Ma.

'Ma, there's something you need to know. Your husband arranged to have our John murdered.' She made a strange gurgling sound and collapsed into the dirt. Buggeration! He shouldn't have told her so bluntly. She were that fond of those boys; hearing such dreadful news were too much for her.

He dropped to his knees, straightened her skirts to cover her dignity, and shook her gently. She were breathing all right, a bit pale, but he reckoned she'd just fainted.

'Ma, Ma, sit up. It's damp down there and you'll ruin your nice gown.'

She stirred and opened her eyes. 'John? Is he dead?'

'No, but it were touch and go. He ain't going to be right in the head after what they did to him.'

He held out his hand and she took it. When she was safely on her feet he brushed the dirt from her skirt and straightened her bonnet. 'There, nobody would know. I'm sorry, I shouldn't have told you like that.'

'Sarah will never forgive me. I had my head turned by him, acted like a silly girl, imagined myself in love with him. The moment the licence was signed he changed. He hurt Sarah, almost killed her, and I couldn't do anything about it.'

'Has he got his hands on the business money?'

'He hasn't. He said I had to sign it over to him but after what he did to my Sarah I refused. He's been beating me, hoping I will give in.'

'Don't you fret, Ma – you'll be a widow soon. The three bastards what attacked our John are dead. He'll be joining them.'

He stiffened at the sound of raised voices. Hatch and at least one other man were outside looking for them. The noise faded and then the welcome clanking of the train approaching meant they could make good their escape. He weren't happy about dodging the bastard but his comeuppance were on its way. Now weren't the time. He needed to get Ma safe.

17

John was able to drink from a cup and swallowed some broth fed to him on a spoon. His eyes were still blank and he didn't react to anyone apart from Spot. Sarah was just glad he was alive.

'Ma, is Uncle Alfie coming back? He weren't here more than a few hours; now he's gone again,' Davie said.

'He had to hand in his resignation at Scotland Yard and go to the bank and so on. He'll be here for tea.'

'I'm sleeping with John from now on. If he needs the po I can lift him on and off. You and Auntie Betty don't need to be in there of a night any more.'

'If you're sure, then that would be a great help. Betty, Ada and I are taking it in turns to sit with him during the day. Why don't you make a start on turning the outbuilding into a carpentry shop? I'm going to see Mr Daniel. I can't understand why the constables haven't been round to speak to me and I'm hoping he'll be able to tell me what's going on.'

There were too many adults living under this roof. They really didn't need three live-in maids as well as the three seamstresses in the attics. At least the girls didn't have to tramp though the house as they had their own staircase. Poor Sally had too many to cook for in the family without having to make meals for the seven girls.

If she could find a two-bedroom cottage close by she would rent it. Sally and Meg could remain here but the other five could move out. Then they would be responsible for their own laundry and the only meal she needed to supply would be at midday. The shop was bringing in double what she'd expected and she was putting a decent amount each week in the bank. On the way out, she would stop and talk to Betty who was working in the shop today.

'I don't reckon they'll want to go, Sarah. They've got it easy here, everything done for them,' Betty said when she spoke to her.

'I won't give them the option to stay. The rent will be paid; I'll give them a bit extra each to pay for their food and heat. We can hardly move in here without falling over one another.'

Ada had just come in from taking the children for a walk and overheard this remark. 'If they don't want to go, I'll take the cottage and get out of your way.'

'You'll do no such thing. You're part of the family as far as I'm concerned and belong here. As I was saying to Betty, we really don't need three servants. Between us we can do everything that needs doing for the children and keep the house spotless.'

'Good thing this is a grand, big house with five bedrooms and two attics.' Ada smiled. 'Are you going to tell them before you rent the cottage or wait until you find what you want?'

'I haven't decided. What I do know is that the family comes first. I have John to take care of and he must be my priority.'

'My Alfie will be here from now on and he and Davie can do the collections and deliveries.'

'I must get on. I don't want to leave him for too long. He's asleep at the moment but will you check on him for me, Ada, if I'm not back within the hour?'

Today she walked up the hill, along High Street and back down Maidenburgh Street instead of taking the quickest route to Mr Daniel's house. It was unlikely she would be attacked but those houses were occupied by men who might work for Hatch.

Meg, the kitchen maid, had taken a note first thing, informing him of her intended visit. It was an imposition asking him to be there to speak to her but she was certain he would do so. He was a good man. Her brother had been lucky to find him to purchase his business.

His dog was flopped on the front step and got up to greet her. He was so like his father – Buster – it brought tears to her eyes. The front door was open and she called out.

'Mr Daniel, thank you for seeing me.'

He had been in the kitchen and stepped into view. 'Come along in, Mrs Cooper. I should have come to see you anyway. There's things you need to know.' He beckoned her forward. 'How's the little lad?'

She found it strange being inside the cottage she had lived in for a while when Alfie and Betty had been here. Most of the furniture was familiar to her as her brother had made it.

'John's conscious. I believe he will not die from his injuries. He's blind and only interacts with the dog. We fear he'll not make a full recovery.'

'I'll make a pot of tea. There's biscuits on the plate. Help yourself. I bought them specially. Don't run to baking, so they'll be safe to eat.'

Whilst he pottered about in front of the range she looked around with interest. Everything was spick and span. Freshly washed laundry danced on the line in the yard. Things smelled different, not unpleasant, but not the same.

'Do you have a horse here?'

He turned with a grin. 'Peggy's out with the cart and one of the boys. The other lad's got the barrow.'

'I am not overfond of equines, Mr Daniel, but I know that having a stable was the reason you bought this property. Whilst we're on the subject of animals – do you know if your dog has fathered a litter of puppies? I would really like to buy one for Alfie as dear Buster died last year.'

'I know of two. When we've had our tea, I'll take you to look at them and you can choose one yourself. My Sinbad's the image of Buster and I can't tell you how pleased I am with him.'

'As you've probably surmised my brother's returned to Colchester. He was working as a police detective, would you believe? I was quite astonished.'

He chuckled. 'A poacher turned gamekeeper – they make the best peelers. I gave my statement to the sergeant at the police station and there's no need for you to make one. The men would have been charged with attempted murder if any of them had survived – and the penalty for that is the noose.'

'I was afraid they would want to shoot the dogs as dangerous. It's a huge relief. They can't be the only three still connected to Hatch, which is why I want another guard dog. Alfie coming back just now is fortuitous. We need a man in the house to protect us.'

'I think you're wise to consider this ain't over. We need to cut the head off the snake to end this.'

Her tea slopped onto the table at his blunt statement. It wasn't that she didn't think Hatch should die for what he'd done, it was the risk to Alfie and Mr Daniel that disposing of him posed. She was certain Davie would be involved too.

'I don't want any of my family implicated with such a thing, or you on our behalf. You could end up dangling on the gibbet and the villain's not worth that.'

'It's not your concern, Mrs Cooper. It's a man's business to protect his family.' He paused. 'I'd thought to find myself a wife but had no success. I was taken with your Sally. Would you object if I courted her?'

'Good heavens, I should be delighted for both of you.' She drained her cup. 'I don't wish to appear impolite, but if I'm to see the puppies I should like to do so now.'

'Both litters are in Northgate Street, not too far. The owners of the bitches both asked for Sinbad and even paid me a few bob for the privilege. Buster was a fine dog, one of a kind, and a lot of folk want one just like him.'

'I can understand that. Davie and Alfie are going to set up a carpenter's shop. They just need to find the necessary tools and purchase some timber. I was hoping that we could make an arrangement for your cart to collect and deliver for us.'

'Just the sort of regular work I like. No need for you to search out tools, I've still got Alfie's in one of the sheds. I'll bring them round tomorrow. Perhaps Sally could have the afternoon off?'

'Of course she can, if she's agreeable. How much do you want for the tools?'

'Nothing – I've just been storing them. They were never part of the deal.'

As they walked to the first location, she told him about her plans for moving the girls from the attic and he nodded. 'I reckon I know exactly the place for you. You don't want to be renting from Hatch, and this property ain't his, it belongs to the church. The tenant died last week. The other two of my lads are busy sprucing it up with a bit of whitewash and such. It's in West Stockwell Street, adjacent to the churchyard.'

'Do you think we could view it today?' She remembered the kindness of the vicar when her little brother Tommy had drowned and her stepfather had turned her out of the house. Through him she had found her position at Grey Friars House.

'Reckon so. This is where the first litter is,' he said, gesturing to the house. 'The pups are ready to go. The second litter were only born two weeks ago.'

The cottage he'd stopped in front of was like all the others in the row. A house with a scrubbed step, spotless curtains and not a smear of dirt on the windowpanes. People around here took pride in their homes.

There was a side alley and he took her down this. She could hear the puppies playing in the yard. He banged on the gate. 'Here, Jonah, got a lady here wants to look at your puppies.'

'Good enough, let yourself in. Mind none of the little buggers escape,' Jonah yelled back.

'Watch where you put your feet, Mrs Cooper,' Mr Daniel said cheerfully as he leant over and unbolted the gate from the inside. He opened it sufficiently for them both to slip through and then shut it quickly.

Immediately she was surrounded by six overexcited puppies. There was no sign of the owner and Mr Daniel nodded towards the privy and winked.

She knew at once which one she was going to take back with her. 'I want this one,' she said as she picked up the wriggling bundle. 'He's identical to Buster, even the same sandy brown colour.' She didn't like to hold a conversation with a man doing his business.

'How much for the big, yellow pup?' Mr Daniel shouted.

'Who's it for? Anyone I know?'

'Alfie Nightingale's sister. Buster died last year…'

'Then you have it, Mrs Cooper. I know why you want it.' There was the sound of scuffling and then the door opened revealing a stooped, elderly man with sharp, intelligent eyes.

'My brother's returned home. He will come and thank you himself.'

The old man nodded. 'What happened to your son weren't right. If a man has a grudge you don't take it out on a child.'

Sinbad had been left outside in the passageway and was scratching the door and whining to get in. 'We'd better get off, Mrs Cooper, before the dog damages the gate. Do you want me to carry the puppy?'

'If you wouldn't mind, I would be grateful. I think we must put off visiting the cottage as we can hardly take a puppy in with us.'

'I'll take the little tyke to your house. You go and speak to the vicar and tell him I sent you.'

The cottage was ideal and she paid three months in advance and went home with the rent book in her bag. It would need furnishing, but this could be the first work that Alfie and Davie took on. The girls could make their own curtains and she could order in the other things they needed. Two days ago her world had fallen apart and now her spirits were lifting and she began to believe the family would get through this. If only Robert and Joe would return – for without them she could never be truly content.

* * *

Chelmsford, August 1849

Ma whimpered and clutched his hand. Alfie held his finger to his lips and she nodded. The voices faded, and he cautiously opened the door as he heard the train approaching.

'Quick, we need to get aboard smartish.' With one hand gripping her elbow and the other holding his bag, he half dragged her through the door, around the corner of the building and onto the platform. Davie's friend had a compartment door open in second class and they tumbled in.

The door slammed. After what seemed like an age the train steamed out of the station.

'Oh, Alfie, he'll not let me go. He's got men in Colchester who will find me and I'll not survive the encounter. He wants my business and my money and as my husband he'll get all of it if I'm dead.'

'I'll get him first, Ma. I've got friends too.'

As the train rocked through the countryside they shared news. Him being a police constable and then a detective made her smile for the first time since he'd seen her.

'Imagine that! Your real pa would be proud of you, proud of both of you. You've overcome adversities and managed to make a success of your lives. I've brought you nothing but trouble and heartache.'

'Marrying that bastard were a bad thing, but you took me and Betty and the boys in without a second thought. Then Sarah and her family joined us and you welcomed them all.'

'I love those boys of hers as if they were my own grandchildren. It must be so hard for my Sarah to have lost Joe and the man she was going to marry.'

'They ain't given up hope, not Ada nor her. If it weren't for the fact that there's been no sighting of the ship at any port they wouldn't be considered lost at sea. They wasn't due back until last month and coming that distance, all the way from India, ships is often months overdue and still turn up.'

'It will be strange returning to Colchester. I want to be known as Mrs Rand again – I won't hear his name spoken by any of you.'

She sat staring out of the window for the remainder of the journey, which allowed him time to rehearse in his head how he was going to explain the fact that he'd brought her to live with them after what she'd done to Sarah and Betty by marrying that bastard.

They disembarked and he carried both bags. 'There wasn't a train when I left Colchester with Jack Rand. We had to travel to London on the common stage. My precious things were sold. When he died I had to sell everything and start again in Chelmsford. I can't credit that I have to do it yet again; this time I've got nothing but the clothes I stand up in and what's in that bag.'

'Did you bring your bank book?'

'I certainly did. I'm going to withdraw all the money and give it to you and Sarah. That way if anything happens to me all he'll get are the premises – and they are leased not owned outright. The business will fail without me there to run it, which is another reason he'll be desperate to find me.'

'Abduction or murder? Make up your mind, Ma. Sarah ain't going to be too happy about seeing you, especially with her John so poorly because of your husband. I won't let her turn you away. Don't look so worried.'

The clock of St Peter's struck five times. He'd said he'd return in time to eat supper with the family and he'd kept his word. He was that desperate to hug his boys, prayed they'd not run away from him as he must be like a stranger to them now.

'Here we are. We'll go in the side door. You stay behind me. In fact, I reckon it might be better if you stayed out here until I've spoken to her.' He'd expected her to argue but she stopped outside the gate without protest. 'I'll not be long. You'd better have your bag.'

He unlatched the gate and stepped in. He almost tripped over a puppy the image of Buster. Then Spot galloped up to join in the fun, hotly pursued by Davie.

'Ma brought him for you. Ain't he grand? What you going to call him?'

Alfie dropped to his knees and scooped up the squirming bundle. 'Well what've we got here? Ain't you a fine little fellow then?' The puppy pissed on his trousers. 'See what you've done now – I won't impress your Auntie Sarah smelling rank.'

He stroked the little dog's head, pulled his ears gently, and then cradled him against his chest. Instantly the puppy calmed, licked his hand and fell asleep.

'Well, look at that. First time he's been quiet since we brought him back an hour ago,' his sister said from the door.

'I'm going to call him Buster after his grandad – it's the best gift I could have had.'

'You should get up – I can hear your boys coming.'

He had no time to move before his sons erupted from the door and flung themselves into his arms on top of the sleeping dog. The puppy wriggled but didn't protest.

'Pa, you've come back.' Tommy smothered him with kisses. Jimmy did the same and then Betty came out to join them. 'Ma, the puppy wet all over our pa,' he said gleefully.

'Puppies do that. Pity we can't put a rag on their backsides.'

Alfie somehow managed to stand up, the puppy and both children still clinging to him.

Sarah pointed to the gate. 'Are you going to leave Ma outside much longer?'

He grinned sheepishly. 'I were going to tell you but then I got distracted. Hatch's been knocking her about. She's scared for her life. I couldn't leave her.'

'Of course you couldn't. Don't bring that leaking puppy inside. He's going to sleep in the workshop with Spot and then you'd better change your trousers.'

This had gone better than he'd dared hope. He'd leave his sister to make her peace with Ma and concentrate on getting to know his boys. What better way to make friends than over a new puppy? The two of them were chattering away. He wasn't following half of it, but Betty answered for him.

'Buster can't stop here on his own. Spot needs to be inside with our John.'

18

Sarah went to the gate and beckoned her mother in. Seeing the bruise and the split lip was enough for her to accept Alfie's decision to bring her here – but the woman wasn't welcome to stay in the house for long. Once things were calmer she would find her mother somewhere else to live. She didn't want her under her roof any longer than necessary.

'Sarah love, thank you for taking me in. I'll...'

'There's no need to thank me. This is Alfie's home as well as mine and it's his wish to have you here. I'll never forgive you for marrying that man, for choosing him over us.'

She turned her back and left the woman she would never think of as her mother standing forlorn in the doorway. As far as she was concerned Alfie had brought back a woman in need of help. God knows where she was going to sleep – the house was overcrowded already and she certainly wasn't sharing with her.

'Please wait in the front parlour until suitable arrangements have been made to accommodate you.' She pointed to the door. 'Go up the three steps and along the passageway.' The unwanted guest made no comment and vanished into the room and closed the door behind her.

Ada was folding linen in the dining room with Sarah's daughter. 'Mary, run along outside and see the puppy and your uncle. Tell them supper will be ready in half an hour.' The child ran off eager to join in the fun. 'Alfie brought my mother back with him. Hatch has been mistreating her. Where is she going to sleep?'

'I'll go in with my three. They've a large room all to themselves. Then she can go in my box room.'

'I hate to put any of us out for her, but I can see no other way around it. I'll get two of the girls to organise that. Until then that woman can remain in the parlour on her own. I'll not have her mixing with the family as if she belongs here.'

If Ada thought her decision harsh she didn't say so. 'I'll tell Meg to take her a tray and then show her where the water closet is and then she can retire early.'

'I'm going back upstairs. Send one of the children to fetch me when the meal is ready.'

The room had a strange odour. It reminded her of her brief stay in the recently constructed county hospital in Lexden Road when she'd been attacked by thieves and Dan had come to her aid. She had spent the afternoon talking to John, reading stories, but got no reaction. He seemed indifferent to her presence and only reacted when the dog was with him.

She stopped, one hand on the banister, one foot on the stairs. The dog must sleep in here with the boys and the puppy couldn't possibly be left alone outside. She didn't want him upstairs until he was house-trained. He would have to sleep on an old blanket in the hallway between the workshop and the house. The flagstone floor would be easy to mop clean in the morning.

Her mother kept away from everyone. Apart from the fact that the front parlour was no longer available to the family and the box room was now occupied by her, one wouldn't have known she was living with them. A week passed and John's sight began to return. He smiled when he had visitors, could indicate when he needed the po and was able to hold a cup. However, he still didn't speak and Sarah wasn't sure he knew who any of them were.

Little Buster was as clever as his namesake and was no longer leaving unpleasant surprises in the hallway. He spent all day in the garden frolicking around with Smoke. The cat had adopted the puppy and seemed to think it was his business to entertain him.

Sarah was certain everyone apart from her and the children spent time with the unwanted guest. Alfie had said it was better for no one to know Ma was living with them. This suited Sarah well enough as it meant she could pretend that woman wasn't under her roof.

The doctor no longer visited. They were to call him if they were concerned about any changes in John's condition and he would return to remove the splints in another few weeks. Three weeks after the attack Alfie carried him down so he could sit in the rocking chair in the dining room and become part of the family again.

'There you are, son, nice and comfy,' she said.

His eyes were brighter. He seemed more alert down here. Slowly he turned his head and then looked at her. 'Ma. Want doggy.'

Her heart leapt. 'Davie will fetch him for you. He's in the garden with Buster.'

She smiled for the first time in weeks. She didn't care if her youngest son never fully recovered; as long as he could communicate his life would be bearable.

The dining room was where they spent all their time now as they could no longer use the front parlour. The clatter of claws on the boards outside heralded the arrival of not just Spot but also the puppy and the cat. These two were now inseparable and slept together in the passageway.

John leant forward and reached out, not for Spot this time, but for Buster.

'Here you are, this is little Buster, Spot's brother.' Davie gently placed the puppy on John's lap and the dog stood on his hind paws and licked John's face.

'Nice doggy, my doggy.' He closed his arms around Buster possessively. She held her breath waiting for the animal to squirm away as he disliked being restrained. Instead he wagged his tail and flopped down and fell asleep.

'Well I never! Just look at that?' Betty said.

'I think I'm going to have to share my gift, Sarah. He ain't said much, but it's a start.'

Mary, Tommy and Jimmy settled down around the rocking chair and John continued to talk, but as if he was Jimmy's age and not nine years old. She drew Alfie to one side leaving Betty to keep an eye on them. Ada had gone to visit a friend for tea and wasn't yet back.

'We should have fetched him down sooner. The difference is quite miraculous.'

'Don't get your hopes up, Sarah love. I don't reckon he'll ever be the boy he was.'

She brushed her eyes angrily. 'I know that. I've known that from the start. He'll be able to run about, can control his bodily functions and tell us what he wants. I'm sad that he will never grow up and have a family of his own, but he can be happy here with us.'

'He'll never be able to do for himself. What happens when we're gone?'

'Then his brothers and sister will take care of him. He'll not end up in an asylum.'

'You said brothers, not brother. You ain't given up hope that Joe and Robert will come back one day?'

'I had almost done so, but after today I truly believe they could still be alive and trying to find their way back to England.' She gestured towards the laughing children. 'Prayers do get answered and miracles can happen.'

'Seeing as John's so much better, can you forgive Ma? She suffered something terrible and she's still part of this family.'

She was about to say no but said something else entirely. 'It's going to take longer to forgive her, but I can't keep her shut away. That's not kind of me. She's grandma to these children, the only one they've got. I can't deny them her love.'

He turned but she shook her head. 'I'll go. We need to have a talk first.'

The parlour door was ajar. She felt a sharp stab of guilt at the thought that Ma had spent the past few weeks only being able to listen from a distance and not talk to her grandchildren. She paused at the door and looked in. The woman sitting in the chair was almost unrecognisable. She had aged, lost so much weight and was pale as a ghost. This was her doing.

'Ma, I'm so sorry. I've been cruel to you. Can you forgive me for my unkindness?'

The change was extraordinary. Suddenly there was colour in Ma's cheeks, her shoulders straightened and she was on her feet holding her arms open. Sarah didn't hesitate. They embraced. Tears were pouring down her cheeks and it was as if a weight lifted from her chest.

'I deserved to be kept here. You took me in; you didn't have to after what I did to you...'

'You were infatuated, tricked by that monster. You did nothing apart from being foolish. It was all him, and I should have understood that from the first.'

She dried her eyes and blew her nose noisily. 'You must see how John's recovered. He'll never be the same, but he's part of the family again and I thank God for that.'

As they were leaving the parlour Ma gripped her arm. 'I don't know if Alfie told you, but I transferred all my money to you and him. If anything happens to me then all that man will get is the business and the lease to the house.'

A shiver of fear at these words ruined her happiness. She'd managed to put aside the fact that Hatch was still out there, probably plotting at this very moment to get his revenge.

* * *

Alfie hadn't been idle these past three weeks. He'd been visiting Richard Daniel most days. His sister and wife thought he was organising their new business arrangement but that was only part of it. Together they were trying to come up with a scheme to do away with that bastard, end his miserable life, but do it so they wouldn't be suspected.

This weren't proving an easy task. 'I don't want me nephew involved, Richard. It's got to be the two of us.'

'Right enough, Alfie. Arriving in Chelmsford on the train we'd be seen and remembered – there ain't enough passengers disembarking there for us to mingle with the crowd, not like in the Smoke.'

'Stagecoach?'

'Even worse – there ain't more than half a dozen passengers on one of them. We've got to lure him to Colchester. He still owns a dozen or more properties around here. What if we cause problems for him? Wouldn't he come personal like to sort them out?'

'He might, but he's still got half a dozen men in his employ. I reckon he'd use them. I can't see we can do anything that they couldn't stop.'

'What about Ma? He'd come in person if he knew she was with us.'

'You can't use her as bait, Alfie lad. That ain't right.'

'I weren't suggesting that. If you let slip in one of the beerhouses what them lot drink in that she was living in that cottage me sister has rented, wouldn't he come himself to fetch her back?'

'He might, but he's more like to send his henchmen to do her in.' His friend scratched his head and poured them both another mug of tea. It were still strange sitting in the kitchen of what used to be his own home. 'You can't put them lasses into danger.'

'They won't be moving in for another week or so. What if we leave clues for him to find? Make it look as if she were there but has moved on again.'

'This needs more thought, Alfie lad. Your timber will be arriving at your drum shortly and you'll want to be there to unload it, won't you?'

'I'll be getting along then. We'll both give it some thought.'

His friend stood up and rammed his cap on his head and tied a muffler around his neck. The weather was closing in, a bite to the air. It would be winter soon.

'You coming with me then?' Alfie grinned. The reason Richard were coming weren't to help him but to spend a few minutes with their cook, Sally. He would be sorry to see the girl go as she were good at her job, but Richard deserved to be happy.

* * *

Colchester, December 1849

The weeks slipped by and John continued to improve physically. The splints had been removed from his arm and leg and he was dashing about the place playing with the little ones as if he were the same age as them.

The three seamstresses and the two maids they had brought with them from Chelmsford were happily established in their cottage and the house was functioning as it should. Ada had taken the four children for a walk to the river and they were now happily eating buns in the kitchen.

'It's turned much colder, there'll be snow tonight, you mark my words,' Ada said as she settled comfortably into a chair in the front parlour.

'And it'll be Christmas soon – our first one here. I want to make it special for everyone. We can afford to – the shop's doing well. The toys Davie and Alfie are making are drawing in the customers too.'

'My boy Fred will be leaving in the new year. I wish he hadn't decided to go to sea, but it must be in the blood as I've now got several sons who've become sailors.'

'I'm glad you brought that subject up. You told me not to give up hope until December – I don't know why but I still believe they'll come home to me eventually.'

'His wages stopped last month so the owners of the vessel have obviously decided they won't return. You must write to them and claim Joe's money – you're entitled to it.'

'I'll do better than that, I'll go to London and take the letter in person. I shall also visit the warehouses and other emporiums. I haven't been since that first time and there will be new products and materials I know nothing about.'

'I don't like the idea of you travelling all that way on your own, Sarah love. Why don't you take Alfie and Betty with you? You could stop overnight, go to the theatre or something, be a real treat for all of you.'

'I'm certain Betty wouldn't want to come; she's sick most days. She thinks she's having a girl this time as she wasn't poorly when she was carrying either of the boys.'

'Doesn't mean you can't ask Alfie. He'll not want you to go alone. Things might have been quiet these past few weeks but it doesn't mean that man has forgotten about you or your ma.'

'Why do you think I've not been attending church or leaving the house?' Her mother had overheard the remark as she came in carrying the tea tray. With only Meg and Sally employed, and they were busy in the kitchen, the daily housekeeping had been taken over by her ma.

'I wish I knew what he was plotting. I don't approve of violence, but in his case I wouldn't be sorry to hear he'd met a nasty end as long as Alfie wasn't involved.'

'Davie told me he's seen men watching this place. If we didn't have the dogs I think they might have attempted to break in one night. They know I'm here; they're just waiting for a chance to murder me.'

'We won't let anything happen to you. You're safe with us. Don't forget we've got Richard Daniel looking out for us as well. After what happened to John, Hatch isn't popular around here with anyone apart from those few men he still has contact with.'

'Alfie said he had a word with the sergeant at the police station and the burglary has stopped.' Ada poured the tea and handed it round.

'Ma, I'm planning to go to London as long as the weather's clement. Ada thinks I shouldn't go on my own.'

'And she's quite right. Take Alfie and Mr Daniel too, if he'll accompany you. That man would hear that you're on the train and send someone after you.'

'I thought to close the shop on Christmas Day and Boxing Day. We should celebrate in style.' Sarah changed the subject and no more was said about the danger of taking a trip to London.

That night she drew her brother to one side and explained why she wished to go to Town. 'Ma's right to be concerned. That bastard ain't given up. I didn't want to worry you, but Richard heard the premises in Chelmsford has gone and Hatch's coming back to Colchester.'

'When? Do you know?'

'Could be back now. I ain't sure. Them lads I used to employ are grown now. With them, me, Richard and Davie we'll deal with him. No problems there.'

Her brother's expression was murderous. He had something planned and she wasn't sure she wished to know what it was. 'I don't want you, any of you, to do anything... anything that will get you arrested.'

'Don't fret, Sarah. I ain't stupid. It'll be done one dark night, no one the wiser but us what did it. With him gone his men ain't going to be any trouble.'

'Surely there's another way? Won't killing him in cold blood make you the same as him?'

His eyes narrowed. For an instant he was a formidable stranger. 'I ain't in the habit of hurting children. Disposing of Hatch will be doing a public service. There won't be no constables looking to arrest no one.'

'I don't want my Davie involved. Is that clear?'

'He ain't going to listen to me, nor you, about this. He's almost full-grown, old enough to make his own decisions. It were his little brother what was maimed.' Alfie took her hands and squeezed them. 'It's got to be done, love. We can't live like this; it ain't right not to be able to go about our business without fear of being attacked.'

'I know – you're right. Does Betty know what you plan?'

He grinned, making him look years younger. 'She'd stick a knife in him herself if she got half a chance. Now, if it ain't snowing tomorrow, I reckon we should go. I'll call in and speak to Richard when we take the dogs out last thing.'

Sarah retired early as they were getting up at five o'clock the next morning. The letter she intended to hand in at the shipping office at the port was written, as was the list of questions she intended to ask. Ma, Betty and Ada knew they were going and she was confident the household would continue to function efficiently in her absence.

It would be Mary's fourth birthday next week and they were going to have a party. The children were already planning the games they were going to play and had given Sally a list of requests for food for the tea. Her daughter's birthday gift was to be a doll. Ada had found this on a market stall and had painstakingly restored the body and face. Then each of them had sewn outfits to match the ones that Mary wore.

It didn't seem quite right to be celebrating so lavishly for this birthday when none of the other children had had a party of any sort. They had all had a gift and a cake but no more than that. Ada had reassured her that her three were delighted to be attending the party and thought it right they should have a bit of a do now John was as good as new – apart from his mind, that is.

19

With his dark topcoat and cap on and his muffler around his face, Alfie reckoned no one would recognise him. His mouth curved under the scarf. With the dogs at his heels, though, it were the same as having a label on his back. Richard had left the side gate open to the yard – no need to close it when you had a dog roaming free. Richard's own dog, another one almost identical to Buster, greeted him enthusiastically.

'You lot stop out here. I'll not be long.' He had already taken his two for a run along the marshes so they didn't need any more exercise.

The back door opened as he went up the steps. 'I've got news for you. I'd have come round to see you if you hadn't come tonight. Sit yourself down. I fetched a jug of beer. You're going to need it when I tell you what I heard.'

Alfie tossed his outer garments onto a chair and sat at the table. No need to take his boots off unless he went into the parlour at the front. 'Hatch is back?'

'Arrived this morning. He's back in his old cottage and had half a dozen ne'er-do-wells in there with him all day. The little lad I employ managed to sneak round the back and get a look in the window. They've got shooters, Alfie. Dogs won't be no use against them.'

'He's insane. He must be to think he can shoot us and get away with it.

I'm going to London – it's what I came round to tell you – for Sarah to make enquiries at the port and visit the warehouses nearby. I ain't happy to leave the house unprotected. Would you spend the day there in my absence?'

'I'd be happy to. I'll be there first thing. I made sure the peelers know about the guns. They'll be keeping a close eye on them bastards. I reckon your family will be safe enough if they go a different route. Stay away from Stockwell Street, and don't go out at night.'

Alfie drained his mug of beer and wiped his mouth on his sleeve. 'I'll be getting on then. I'll go the long way around – along High Street and then down North Hill. Good thing I fetched the leads for me dogs. They ain't walking loose with all the traffic.'

It was good practice for the animals to walk beside him. He was going to have to do that tomorrow. He weren't too sure about this trip, not now, but with Richard in the house they should be safe enough.

* * *

'Betty love, I'm off now. Don't none of you go out the house today.' Alfie weren't sure his wife had heard him, but Richard would be there to remind her. She were right poorly with this babe, not like the other times. Sarah had told him about Dan's first wife. Betty had taken so quick – the first night he'd come back, he reckoned. When this one arrived he'd not share her bed. He'd rather do without than risk losing his Betty. He was wearing his smart togs and snatched up his top hat as he crept out of the room.

His sister had a pot of tea and toast waiting in the kitchen. Sally and Meg didn't start for another hour.

'It didn't snow, Alfie, but there's a sharp frost.' She looked at him and her expression changed to concern. 'What's wrong? Why do you look so grim?'

He told her what he knew. 'If he's here then there's no need to take the dogs. They will be better in the garden protecting the family. We'll be in London before Hatch or his men are awake.'

'I'll leave a note for Davie asking him to walk the dogs...'

'No, they can do their business in the yard. He can clean it up. It won't matter for one day.'

He turned as the boy walked in – well – not a boy no longer, almost a man. 'John's sound asleep. I heard you get up. Is there tea in the pot, Ma?'

She poured a cup and then handed him the toasting fork and a slice of bread to hold in front of the flames on the range. 'Did you hear your uncle, Davie? Hatch is back and you must stay inside where it's safe today. No deliveries.'

'Mr Daniel will be here soon. You let him in when he gets here,' Alfie said.

Her son grinned. 'Won't need to do that, Uncle Alfie – Sally's always got an eye out for him. I reckon you'll get to speak to the governor looking like you do. If I didn't know better, I'd think you were grand folks.'

They went out through the shop and Davie locked it up again after them. It were still dark but the streets were well lit with gas lamps. The brisk walk to the station warmed them up. There were a dozen or so passengers waiting for the first train.

'I ain't looking forward to being bounced around. My arse were black and blue last time.'

'You should have bought first class. They have padded seats in there.'

The two of them huddled together in the compartment. There were ice on the inside of the window and he was glad he'd put on gloves. 'I'll be happy to get out of this rattletrap. We'll travel with the gents on the way back.'

'Then it's a good thing we didn't bring the dogs.'

They walked to the docks, which wasn't far from the station.

'I've been thinking, why don't I visit the warehouses whilst you take my letter to the port? We can meet at that coffee house over there; ladies are welcome and they have a separate parlour for them to sit.'

Alfie drew out his pocket watch. 'It's just after nine o'clock – how long will it take you to complete your purchases and orders?'

'I shall take a hackney carriage, but it will still take me half an hour to get there. Shall we say midday? There's a train to Colchester at one o'clock, which we can catch and be home before dark.'

He waited with his sister until she were safely in the cab and then strode off to the docks. He'd get this done first and then go in search of Fred. With luck his friend would be on days and his beat would take him past the docks at some point.

The harbour master's office were locked. There were no message pinned to the door to say when the cove would be back. He had no option but to linger until he could deliver the letter. There were several ships being unloaded and he found himself a seat on an upturned barrel to watch.

He were cold sitting still after half an hour and decided to make enquiries as to the whereabouts of the harbour master. There weren't even a letter box he could shove the envelope through. A group of three weather-beaten sailors, their kitbags over their shoulders, had swayed down the gangplank a while back and were now standing, frustrated, looking at the closed door.

'Begging your pardon, mister, do you know where to find him?'

'Ain't got no notion. He must be on a ship somewhere. We need to speak to him before we head off. Bloody cold here – I'd forgot what winter was like.'

'There's a coffee stall over there. Can I treat you to a hot drink?' Alfie didn't know why he'd offered, but there was something about these men that fascinated him. His father had died at sea and he'd always been interested in speaking to those men what travelled so far away.

'That'd be kind of you. We ain't got any rhino. We worked our passage, didn't get paid.' The sailor nodded towards the locked office. 'We need to ask for enough to get us home. We're owed that much after what we've been through.'

They warmed their hands on the tin mugs and he sent an urchin to purchase hot meat pasties for the three of them. 'What ship were you on? My sister's man and son were on *The Empress*...'

'Bugger me! We was on her when she foundered. Half the crew perished, the rest of us lost everything and it's taken us nigh on eight months to get back to England.'

'Me nephew were a cabin boy, Joe Cooper. Robert Billings were first mate.'

The speaker slapped him on the back so hard the tin mug flew from

Alfie's grip. 'Well I never! They both survived and got passage on a ship same time as us. It was docking at Liverpool. I reckon they won't be far behind us.'

The owner of the coffee stall swore and stomped off to recover his property. 'Sorry, fill them up again for us.' He tossed the coins and the man nodded, his anger forgotten.

'I'm here to get news for me sister but I never thought it would be this. She never gave up hope, but it's been a year since she was told the boat went down and she'd lost both of them.' He drained the second mug and put it back on the stall. He dipped into his inside pocket and removed some coins. 'Here, this should be enough to see you home.' He handed them a golden guinea – but he were that pleased with the news he'd have given them every penny he had.

'You're a gent and no mistake, mister. Who'd have thought you'd be here the very day we docked. You should have your family home for Christmas.'

Alfie shook hands with each of them and they parted on the best of terms – the three old salts happy they'd got sufficient to get them home, and a few shillings extra, and he with news he could hardly wait to share with Sarah.

He had two hours to find Fred, ample time even if he had to go to Leman Street to look for him.

* * *

Sarah was delighted with her visit to the various warehouses and, as an established customer, she was now able to buy on credit and pay at the end of each month.

'Your goods will be delivered well before Christmas, Mrs Cooper, depending on the weather,' the clerk told her as he handed her the delivery note.

'That's good news. Remember to include the swatches we talked about – my customers like to be able to select from the latest materials.'

'The crinoline is all the rage; are you sure you don't wish to purchase the necessary whalebone to make the petticoat?'

'My premises are too small to accommodate such a fashion. Good heavens, I should only be able to display one gown if I used the hooped skirt. No, if a lady in Colchester wishes to adopt that style she will have to go elsewhere.'

The weather had improved, the temperature higher in London than at home. It was still cold enough to dampen the noxious smells and make the visit less unpleasant than last time. A church clock nearby struck eleven. She hailed a cab and arrived at the designated meeting place in good time.

She was drinking coffee, not something they had at home, and eating a tasty slice of cake when her brother burst in. One look at his face was enough for her to leap to her feet and rush to meet him.

'Robert and Joe are alive. They're on a ship that should be docking in Liverpool any day and with luck will be home for Christmas.'

Tears coursed down her cheeks and she fell into his arms. They cried with joy together. Eventually they stepped apart to find a waiter hopping from foot to foot trying to attract their attention.

'I beg your pardon, sir, but this chamber is for ladies only.'

'As my sister is the only one present, I'm sure it cannot matter for the moment. Fetch us a jug of coffee and whatever pastries have been baked this morning.' He tossed the man a coin and this did the trick.

'Of course, sir, as long as you are prepared to vacate the premises if another lady comes in, then I'm sure the proprietor will not mind this once that the rules are broken.'

Sarah was incredulous when she heard how Alfie had learnt the news. 'I do believe the good Lord has been listening to our prayers. How else could you have been there at the very time those three sailors disembarked?'

'I'm not a religious cove, as you know, but after this I ain't so sure. I was thinking that we could send Davie to Liverpool with money for Robert and Joe. If he leaves tonight I reckon he'll get there sometime tomorrow. There's trains to the north nowadays.'

'A kind thought, but I doubt he'd find the right dock and he'd have a wasted journey. Robert's a resourceful man – he will get them both home one way or another. What does concern me, however, is that they'll both go to Chelmsford. Davie would be better taking a letter there for his friend to deliver when they turn up.'

'I couldn't find me friend Fred Brown – he's left too. No one knows where he's gone, which is a right shame as I'd like to have kept in touch with him.'

'You have Richard Daniel as your friend nowadays – you don't need another one.'

The waiter brought what he'd ordered and left them to it.

'I shall get the banns called this weekend. I want to be married as soon as Robert gets home.' Her cheeks coloured and she smiled. 'He will be sharing my bed whatever the circumstances.'

'Then it's best you get things organised. I'll get the vicar to visit us – I ain't having you wandering about the place at the moment. Will you look for a house for yourselves in the new year?'

'Not immediately – in the spring perhaps. Ada's boy is going to sea after Christmas. Annie and Beth could move in with Ada. Then Ma can have the vacant room – she's not complained, but I'm sure she would prefer to be out of the box room and into somewhere more comfortable.'

'Ma can stay with us when you do go. She'll be able to keep an eye on Betty in case she gets ill after the baby's born like what she did with our Tommy.'

'I was hoping you would offer to keep her with you. We are on good terms now, but I shall never be entirely comfortable around her after what happened.'

'I reckon Betty and I'll have to take in lodgers. The house will be too big for us when you've left.' Something else occurred to him. 'Will you take Sally and Meg?'

'Sally will be leaving to marry Richard soon so she would have to be replaced anyway. I can't think about all that now. I want to get home and give my boys and Ada the good news.'

* * *

During the next few days the house was cleaned from top to bottom in expectation of the arrival of Robert and Joe. It was eighteen months since she had seen either of them and her son would have grown from a boy to a man in this time.

The vicar had called and the banns had been read. If Robert arrived in time they could be married the week before Christmas. But first they had Mary's anniversary party, which was to be held the next day.

'Ma, there's Billingses, Coopers, Nightingales and a Rand living under this roof and all of us related,' Davie said one evening as they were sitting quietly in the front parlour.

'I hadn't realised there were so many names. I wish John understood that his big brother is coming home at last. Do you think he will recognise Joe?'

'He might. It's a tragedy what happened to him. He ain't never going to grow up – he'll always be a little boy.'

'It's sad, but you must remember he doesn't realise what he's lost. He's content, and between us we can make sure he has a full and happy life.'

Alfie was helping Betty put the boys to bed. Her sickness hadn't abated and she was finding life miserable at present. Ma and Ada were now the best of friends and busy finishing off the last of the outfits for Mary's birthday doll. Ada's children rarely came into the parlour, although they were welcome to, and preferred to spend their leisure time in the dining room.

'Davie, have you heard anything about what Hatch is planning? I'm finding it unnerving that he hasn't made a move.'

'He ain't going to come around here firing his shooters, Ma. He can't do nothing to us if we keep ourselves safe like what we're doing at the moment.'

'I pray that you're correct. Alfie's planning something with you and Mr Daniel, but I don't want to know what it is. He gave me his word that you'd be in no danger and that will have to be good enough for me.'

'We thought to wait until Uncle Robert and Joe are back. It'll even the odds like.'

'Please, tell me no more. I'm going to check on John. He was overexcited about the party tomorrow.'

* * *

Alfie was relieved only Davie was still up when he eventually got downstairs. 'We need to talk, son. I've heard things today what worry me.'

'Me too, Uncle Alfie. One of Mr Daniel's lads heard that bastard plans to burn us out one night.'

'That's what I heard too. I reckon the dogs would smell smoke before we would. It wouldn't take much to set this place alight, what with all the beams and such. I reckon we need to take it in turns to stay up and keep watch. I'll take tonight; you go on to bed.'

The boy hesitated. 'We'd never get everyone out alive – not if they blocked the doors.'

'Richard's let the peelers know so the constables will be walking past here regular like.' He put his arm around Davie's shoulders and hugged him. 'Nothing bad's going to happen – we've had our share of cruel luck. Our Joe's on his way here. That's a sure sign things are looking up.'

He padded in his stocking feet through the house, checking every window was fastened and all doors bolted and locked. Satisfied the house was secure, he settled down on the sofa in the parlour where he could hear anyone walking past on the pavement outside. The dogs were guarding the rear of the house.

It were a long night but he heard nothing untoward. Today were his niece's fourth birthday. They had plenty to celebrate; today an anniversary and in a week or two hopefully a wedding. He'd already got a fine tree to put up in here on Christmas Eve. It were going to be a special time for all of them as long as that bastard didn't do anything to spoil things.

Betty hadn't been sick like this with the boys. It were pitiful to watch her retching so often and getting thinner rather than fatter. Ma and Ada had said this would pass as the pregnancy progressed, but his poor love had another few weeks of misery before this happened. No point in asking her to eat any of the party food, which were a shame and no mistake.

Meg was down raking out the range. He'd take the dogs down the river for a bit. No one was going to be around so early. It were still pitch-dark out.

20

'Tea for you, Mr Nightingale, nice and hot.'

Alfie opened his eyes and saw Meg holding out a steaming mug for him. 'Thank you – just what I needed. You don't look surprised to see me here.'

'No, best to be vigilant. Mind you, no one would've come out last night. Have you looked out the window?'

He grinned. 'Not much point. It's coal-black out there still.'

'It ain't – it's all white. Snowed something cruel last night. There must be six inches of the nasty white stuff.'

'Then for our safety's sake I reckon I'll be glad if it stops for a week or two. Mind you, won't be good for business.'

He drank his tea with enjoyment and headed for the WC to relieve himself. It were a grand thing having an indoor privy – going down the yard in this weather would be unpleasant. Neither dog did more than thump their tail on the floor. How the hell did they know it were thick snow outside? Usually they was eager to go out.

It were too early to disturb Betty so he'd get the fires going around the house, one less job for Meg. Would Ada's children have to go to school today? He didn't want them to get the strap for staying away when the rest of the children turned up snow or not.

Fred was finished with education in two weeks, so it didn't make no never mind if he didn't go again. Beth was happy to stay home and help her mother. It were different for Annie. She were a clever little thing and said she wanted to be a schoolmistress. He didn't think she'd stay home, not for a bit of snow.

By the time the smell of bacon drifted through the house the fires were lit and the older children were downstairs in Ada's care.

'We ain't going in this, Ma,' Fred said. 'I've been out and it's knee-deep in places.'

'I don't like snow, Ma, so I'll stay home this once,' Annie agreed.

'Then we can have Mary's party at lunchtime instead. Don't forget to bid her a happy birthday when she comes down.'

Alfie rubbed his chin. He needed a shave, but that would have to wait until Betty was up. He checked and she was sleeping soundly. As soon as she woke she would be sick so the longer she stayed as she was the better. Sarah was in with the little ones and from the sound of it they were all excited – snow was an adventure for them. Not for the children without shoes. He weren't a radical, but something should be done to help them little ones.

* * *

'I'm not going to open the shop today, Betty. I can't see that any customers will venture out with so much snow and more falling all the time.'

'Alfie said we're safer whilst it lasts, but it's going to make it harder for your Robert and Joe to get back.'

'I don't mind how long it takes now I know they will be here eventually. You look a little better today. Do you think you could eat a slice of toast with your tea?'

'I could, in fact I think I might have two. For the first time in a month my stomach is settled. Ada said it would last until I was halfway through and I'm only a couple of months along.'

'It's what my ma said as well, but not every pregnancy is the same. Listen to that – the children are enjoying a snowball fight in the garden. Mary will never forget this birthday.'

Once everyone was in dry clothes they gathered in the dining room for the celebration tea. It mattered not that they were eating dainty sandwiches, sausage rolls and cake at midday instead of enjoying a hot meal.

Her daughter was overjoyed with her gifts and was more interested in dressing and undressing her doll than playing blind man's buff, hide-and-go-seek or pin the tail on the donkey. The workshop was eerily quiet and there had only been one cart go past all day.

The trains wouldn't run and until the snow stopped and the lines were cleared so there was no chance of Robert or Joe returning. In some ways it made things easier as she was no longer jumping every time she heard a door bang just in case it was them.

The house was quiet by seven o'clock. Even the older three had retired exhausted after the raucous games both inside and out that had occupied the day. Even John had enjoyed himself, had run around laughing and clapping. He wasn't lame. His arm had healed perfectly so he had the full use of it. The fact that he could see perfectly well again was little short of a miracle. They had all accepted he would never recover his faculties. He would remain a little boy in his mind for ever.

Hatch and his men deserved to die for what they'd done to her precious boy. If only they could find some evidence to convict them then the law could serve justice. She wasn't comfortable with Alfie taking matters into his own hands, but he was the man of the house and she must let him make decisions like this for himself.

The snow blanketed the town for another three days and even the children were eager to see it melt so they could resume their normal lives. She had set them to shovelling it from the pavement outside the house and shop entrance, and when that was done they cleared all the way to the back door.

'Things will go back to normal now, Betty. Your assistant and my seamstresses have turned up this morning. I cannot tell you how pleased I am that you are now feeling well.'

'I've never felt better, Sarah. My Alfie was that worried. He's a new man now.'

'I could not help but overhear his eagerness last night; could I ask you to remember to close your door at night in future?' She laughed as she spoke and Betty blushed.

'It's knowing we can do it whenever we want without fear of me catching on that makes it...'

'Please, I am a lonely widow. Do not tell me any more about your bedtime pleasures.'

'Robert will be here any day, then you'll be the one keeping us awake.'

It was her turn to colour. 'So Alfie told you I intend to share my bed without the benefit of clergy? We can marry the week after next so, if I did start a babe, no one would be any the wiser about its conception.'

'I'm glad that Davie and Alfie continued to work during the snow as their wooden toys are proving popular. It might seem odd to some that a haberdasher's and ladies' clothing emporium is also selling little trains and carts.'

'We would be foolish not to have them in the window with the festive season almost upon us, and the well-to-do looking for gifts for their children. The kites are proving particularly successful, which is strange as they are something for summer use.'

Betty had spread butter and marmalade on her toast whilst they were talking and devoured both slices. This was the first time she had eaten anything apart from naked toast. As her friend was licking her fingers she stopped and her eyes widened. For a horrible moment Sarah thought she was going to lose her breakfast but instead she laughed.

'I am well. In fact, I am ravenously hungry. If you will excuse me I'm going to the kitchen to see if there's any of that delicious bacon left over and I shall ask Sally to cook me some eggs as well.'

Annie had gone to school but Beth and Fred were helping Alfie. The two girls who worked as shop assistants had opened the door and there were already two ladies making purchases.

She hadn't banked the weekend's takings and didn't like to have so large a sum of money in the house. There could be no harm in walking around to the bank as long as she stayed on the busy thoroughfares and didn't venture into the narrow streets where Hatch still held sway.

John saw her putting on her boots. 'John come too, Ma. John like outside with Ma.'

She was about to refuse but then reconsidered. He hadn't been away from the house since his near-death experience and it would do him good to view the world with his changed perception. 'Can you fetch your boots, your coat, cap and muffler for me? I shall tell Uncle Alfie that you're coming with me.'

He ran off chattering to himself like little Jimmy did and she headed for the workshop. The snow was piled on either side of the path and showed no sign of thawing. The sky was a clear, bright blue and had none of the heavy grey clouds that gave warning of further snowfall.

She explained to her brother and he nodded. 'Take Spot. He can wait outside with John when you go inside.'

'The paths are icy still. Holding the leash might well pull me from my feet. Thank you, but I'll not take him this time.'

John was happy to put his gloved hand in hers, not something he would have done before that dreadful day. 'It's very slippery out here, John, so we must be extra careful not to fall over.'

There were few vehicles on the hill as it would be too difficult for them to travel in the ice and snow, but there were a goodly number of pedestrians. All of them were muffled in thick winter clothing, hats pulled down over their ears and coat collars turned up.

After checking her son's buttons were done correctly they stepped out into the freezing street. John hopped from foot to foot and his head swivelled as he saw his surroundings so changed. He had seen snow before, but obviously could no longer recall this. Then he pointed, snatched his hand away from hers and started to run headlong down the hill.

* * *

Alfie wasn't happy about Sarah and John going out without protection even though they were only going to walk round to the bank in Head Street.

'Davie, you keep an eye on the lads, see they don't slice off their fingers with the chisel or the plane. I'm going after me sister. I'll not be long. I'll take the dogs – they could do with a run after I've got Sarah and John home safe.'

He was already wearing a heavy topcoat, muffler, and fingerless gloves as it were perishing in the workshop. It weren't safe to have a fire with so much sawdust and such around. He brushed off the worst and then whistled for the dogs. Spot would walk to heel without a leash but it were best to have Buster secure as he were likely to run after cats or other dogs if he spotted any.

He were no more than a few minutes after Sarah and as he pulled the gate shut behind him he heard John cry out and then the child raced past the end of the passageway. Alfie moved so fast his feet almost slid out from under him and he only stayed upright by good luck.

As he reached the pavement Sarah ran past. Something was up and no mistake. Spot was off like a rat from a drainpipe and he too vanished down the hill. Alfie increased his pace and his heart was thundering. He could think of only one thing that had caused such excitement.

He stepped onto the path and saw a few yards away his best friend embracing his sister and his nephew Joe on his knees holding John. The dog was dancing around them barking and his eyes filled. He broke into a run, skidded to a halt beside the two he'd thought lost forever.

Robert was too busy kissing Sarah to take notice of his arrival. Joe got to his feet with his brother still clinging to his neck as if he were indeed a little 'un.

'Joe, I scarce recognised you. I reckon you've grown a foot since I last saw you.' He threw his arms around the youth. He weren't a boy any more, his cheeks wet.

'Uncle Alfie, I can't tell you how glad I am to be back. I know all about John – it's a crying shame. I can't believe he still remembers me after all this time.'

Sarah raised her head. 'He saw you first. I'm not sure I'd have known you immediately if he hadn't run off. We can't stay here blocking the path and making a spectacle of ourselves – we'll go back to the house and you can tell us how you come to be here.'

John refused to walk and Joe was more than strong enough to carry him. Robert and Sarah were still entwined. He'd never seen her look so happy, happier even than when she'd married Dan all those years ago.

'Go down the side. I never got a chance to bolt the gate behind me so it's open.'

Joe laughed, his teeth white in his nut-brown face, and dashed on ahead. Both Davie, Ada and Fred were waiting to greet them.

They sat in the kitchen and he watched with amazement as Robert and Joe consumed enough for half a dozen men before they were satisfied. Both were stick-thin, but nothing good food wouldn't put right in time.

'Robert love, I brought your clothes when I moved here. Sarah's moved them to her closet. Your brothers have been setting up a bath for you. I reckon it'll be done by now.'

He grinned and raised an arm to his nose and pulled a face. 'We both stink – no need to remind us. I hope there's a bath for Joe as well, and something decent to change into.'

Sarah smiled. 'Of course there is. Joe, you'll have to borrow things from Alfie until we can make you fresh garments. I'll get the girls started on shirts and underwear at once. I'll need your measurements for trousers, waistcoats and jackets.'

'Don't try and take them now, Ma. Wait until I'm clean again.'

Sarah led Robert upstairs and into her bedroom. If he thought this forward of her, then too bad. They'd wasted enough time already. The large galvanised tin bath stood steaming in front of the fire. There were half a dozen towels on a rack beside it.

'Get those clothes off. I'll burn them on the range downstairs.'

He raised an eyebrow and then laughed. 'Right you are. This wasn't how I imagined things would be when we finally shared a bed, but...'

She put her hands on her hips and pursed her lips as if shocked at his comment. 'You're getting ahead of yourself, Robert Billings. I'm here to help you bathe. I don't recall my bed coming into the conversation.'

He laughed and this sent ripples of pleasure from her toes to her crown. 'I'm literally half the man I was when I left here eighteen months ago, but every ounce of me belongs to you.'

'I've had the banns called. We can get married next week.'

'In which case, there's no more to be said. If you're here to help, woman, why are you standing so far away?'

Although he was painfully thin, he was strong and she ached to be in his arms, but not until he smelt better and she had scrubbed the months of dirt from his person.

He kept his back to her and stepped into the water. She knew why this was and hoped his ardour would remain strong once he was clean again.

Just doing something as mundane as scrubbing his back was a joy. Her gown was soaked by the time she was done. He stood up, unashamedly naked, and then wrapped himself in the largest of the towels.

'You need to change your gown, my love, and I am still waiting for my fresh garments.'

'I am already failing dismally in my wifely duties.' She turned to face him and with slow deliberation stepped out of her sodden dress. She stooped to collect the hem of her petticoats but he was there before her. He didn't bother with the laces or the buttons but tore them apart.

When she woke hours later entwined in his arms the room was dark apart from the flickering of the coal in the fire. The fact that everyone in the household would know what they'd been doing all afternoon bothered her not one jot. She was where she was meant to be, in the arms of the man she loved and thought she'd lost.

She fell asleep again and was woken when he scrambled out of bed. 'Where are you going?'

'I need to talk to Alfie, darling. Go back to sleep.'

* * *

Alfie spent the afternoon in the workshop finishing off the last of the toys to go into the shop window. He'd sent word round to Richard to come at eight o'clock. Robert was otherwise occupied with Sarah but would be down by then.

After the excitement and celebrations the house were eventually quiet. He sent Meg and Sally to their beds as well leaving the kitchen for his meeting.

Richard arrived on time. 'Bugger me, it's perishing out there. No sign of a thaw.'

Joe and Davie were already at the table. All they needed were for

Robert to join them. There was a mug of tea in front of each chair. Once the three of them were settled he began proceedings.

'I ain't spending another day watching me back and wondering what that bastard's going to do. We get rid of him, permanent like, then we can easy scare the others away.'

'They'll make their move as soon as the snow's thawed,' Richard said.

'Then we'd better do it soon. It'll have to be when the womenfolk are asleep – best they don't know what we're about,' Alfie replied.

The sound of footsteps approaching meant Robert was finally up. His friend came in. He nodded and took his place without comment.

'We was just saying, we need to strike first. Kill the bastard and bury his body.'

'I can think of a better way than that. We don't want blood on *our* hands if we can help it. This is what I think we should do.'

He listened and when Robert had finished explaining Alfie thumped the table. 'No time like the present. We'll do it tonight.'

The others agreed and half an hour later they were muffled up, their faces obscured, making their way to Hatch's cottage. With the three dogs, and five of them, they should have no difficulty.

Their feet crunched the snow, the noise loud in the silent darkness. Richard and Joe had gone to fetch a large trunk and meet them there. The dogs were running loose, stopping to sniff the air every few yards before trotting ahead. If there were any dangers, they'd have fair warning.

There were to be no talking – voices carried in the night-time. Davie, the smallest and nimblest of the group, went ahead to see what was what. It were possible there was guards. If there was, they'd be armed so best to take precautions.

Every cottage was in darkness – no one awake to see them pass. He didn't reckon anyone would tittle-tattle even if they saw. Since what had happened to John, Hatch were even less popular than he were before. With that bastard gone Ma would own half a dozen cottages, as she were still his legal wife even if she didn't use his name no more.

Davie returned as quietly as he'd gone. He didn't speak, just raised his fist and nodded. Alfie had brought a couple of things what would be useful to break in. They'd need to do it swiftly, not give Hatch time to raise the alarm.

The back door would be bolted and locked as would the front. The kitchen window would be the easiest to open. Davie took the chisel and he and Robert lifted him up so he could reach. Seconds later it were done. They pushed and the lad disappeared.

The back door swung open moments later. Before he could move, the dogs were into the house. There was a faint cry and then nothing. It come from upstairs. He pounded up and from the faint flicker of the dying fire he saw their quarry pinned to the bed. They hadn't ripped him to shreds, which were fortunate.

Robert removed several strips of cloth and the man what had caused so much distress to his family were trussed and gagged and ready to be transported. He were still in his nightshirt. Alfie were tempted to take him like he were, but jerked his thumb towards the clothes piled haphazardly on a chair. Joe didn't need telling twice and gathered them up and even remembered to collect the boots as well. These items were shoved into a sack.

The trunk was open in the yard. Joe put the clothes in first, might make it a bit more comfortable, but he doubted it. Then the young man punched their captive on the side of the head and the body went limp. They'd decided it would be easier if the man inside the trunk were unconscious.

He grabbed one handle and Richard took the other. Robert and his nephews would put things back like what they'd been so no one would know anyone had entered the house illegally. They would also pack a bag with personal items, make it look as if Hatch had gone away.

The cove were bloody heavy and by the time they staggered into Richard's yard he were almost done. They dumped the trunk in the shed and locked the door. The horse in the stable whickered, unused to being disturbed in the middle of the night.

'I'll be here with Robert and Joe first thing to get it on the cart.'

'A good night's work. I pray the next part goes as smoothly.'

21

Sarah stirred slightly as Robert slid in beside her. His arms drew her close and she was roused from her sleep. 'You're icy. Have you been out?'

'A bit of business to attend to – nothing for you to worry about. Go back to sleep, my love. The less you know the better for you.'

This was enough to make her pull away and push herself upright. 'Don't you dare exclude me from whatever punishment you're giving to that man.'

There was a significant pause before he responded. 'I'm not telling you tonight, Sarah, but I give you my word when it's done you'll be told everything.'

'Very well, I'll settle for that. As long as we can start living normally again, I don't care what is done to him. He deserves everything he gets. Once he's gone we'll not be the only ones glad to see the back of him.'

He gathered her close again but they did not sleep for a while longer. The next time she awoke she was alone and it was almost seven o'clock. She was tardy and should get dressed immediately. On reflection she decided she would wash thoroughly before dressing. In the circumstances it seemed the sensible thing to do.

Davie came in through the back gate with the dogs and he was smiling. There was no sign of Alfie, Joe or Robert. The house was different today, as if a pall of gloom had been lifted. Ada's son Fred was back and forth with deliveries that had been held up by the snow and the circumstances.

The sun was out and the temperature began to rise. With luck the snow would be gone in a day or two and her customers would return to make last-minute purchases before the holiday season.

She joined Ada, Betty and the children in the dining room mid-morning. For some reason Ma didn't join them. 'I must select an outfit for my wedding day. There's not time to make something new even if I wished to do so.'

'The moss green skirt with the matching jacket and high-necked lace blouse would be perfect. You even have a bonnet to match,' Betty suggested.

'Then that's what I shall wear. I don't want a wedding breakfast, or any fuss made on the day. It will be two days before Christmas. I thought we could make it a double celebration.'

'Sally has already been baking. The figgy pudding is done and she has just to ice the cake. She's also made gingerbread stars and the children have put sugar paste on as decoration. They will look perfect on the tree when it goes up on Christmas Eve.' Betty helped herself to another generous slice of plum cake. She was certainly making up for her previous lack of appetite these past two days.

'Have you seen your ma today? Is she in the shop or the workshop?' Betty asked.

'I haven't. I've a notion why she's absent, but I sincerely hope I'm wrong.'

Her mother wasn't downstairs. Surely she wasn't still abed? She hurried up and paused outside the door and could hear her mother crying pitifully. Sarah threw open the door. 'If you wish to remain under my roof you will not cry for that man. Do I make myself clear?'

'I know he's wicked, that he mistreated me and you, and had your son half murdered, but I loved him once. Alfie will kill him and it will break my heart. I pleaded with my boy to allow me to speak to my husband, persuade him to sell up his cottages and move far away from here, but he ignored me.'

'So, these past weeks have been a pretence? If you were so sure of your feelings, why didn't you go to him?'

Her mother sniffed loudly and blew her nose on the sheet. 'I didn't realise that I still loved him despite his wickedness until Alfie and the others went out to murder him last night.'

'Then, if that's the case, you are now his widow and will inherit his estate. I suggest that you move immediately to his vacant cottage. You're not welcome here.'

No sooner had she said the words than she thought them harsh. Her mother was weak, easily influenced, not truly bad.

'Then I shall be glad to go. I shan't inform the constables, but I don't wish to live with anyone who can kill another human being in cold blood.'

'That is exactly what Hatch tried to do and yet you were ready to forgive him, leave everything and run away to be at his side.'

'And another thing, you are sharing a bed with a man before you've spoken your vows. You're a fallen woman – at least I got married before I did that.'

Sarah had heard quite enough of this nonsense. 'If you pack your belongings, I'll get someone to escort you immediately.'

Her mother's expression changed to horror. 'Please, I didn't mean it. I don't want to live in that little cottage on my own when I can be here with all of you.'

'I'll let the men of the house decide what happens to you. Even if Alfie allows you to stay, you'd do well to keep out of my way in future. You might be my flesh and blood but Ada is more a ma to me than you've ever been.'

The morning dragged. She tried to fill her time with business matters, plans for Christmas, but she was constantly looking at the clock and towards the door in the hope that Robert and the others might return. Had they been arrested? If they were found in possession of a dead body it would be the noose for them all.

* * *

There were a few passengers shivering on the platform waiting for the first train in the icy darkness. The trunk smelt rank – Hatch must have pissed in it. This meant his clothes would be stinking too – served him right. He were lucky he weren't already on the way to hell.

Joe had given the guard a bribe so he looked the other way when they loaded the trunk onto the train. They was travelling third class, less likely to have curious passengers that way. Richard weren't coming with them; he'd got work to do. Robert, Joe and himself could manage even if it meant carrying the bloody thing all the way to the docks.

'Had we better check inside, Uncle Alfie? Not much point in carting a corpse about.'

'No, leave him be. I'll put this rug over it; it'll keep him warm enough. Good thing we brought his bag with us. From the smell he'll need a change of clothes.'

They made themselves as comfortable as possible and despite the inclement conditions Alfie managed to doze off. He was alert when they pulled into Chelmsford, but no one got in third class. They was all ready when the train eventually steamed into the station in London.

The streets was treacherous. Several times they almost dropped their burden, but eventually they arrived at their destination. He were that glad to put the trunk down and leave Joe and Robert to do the rest. Despite the early hour the dock was busy. Ships came and went at all times of the day and night. The area were well lit with lanterns and the occasional gaslight.

The trunk made a decent seat. From the banging and movement Hatch was none the worse for his incarceration. Robert and Joe returned with four seamen who picked up the trunk, balanced the bag on top, and strode away into the darkness.

'Well, that was simple enough. What ship's he on?'

'A Russian trader. They lost three sailors overboard and were only too happy to take Hatch. Didn't have to give them as much as we thought,' Robert said with a smile. 'It's over, Alfie. We can go home and live our lives without fear.'

'Let's get some breakfast before we head back. There's something else we need to discuss.'

Over coffee and a huge platter of eggs, bacon and fried bread they talked about their next move. 'I reckon we can come to an agreement with the tenants of Hatch's cottages. No need for any more violence.'

'Better to leave it until the new year, Alfie. Might seem a bit suspicious if we approach them too soon. They need to believe Hatch has gone willingly,' Robert said.

'Then that's what we'll do. I'll be glad to get home and get a bit of shut-eye. All this gallivanting in the middle of the night ain't for me no more.'

'You was a peeler, Uncle Alfie. You must have been used to being up all night nabbing villains.'

'It seems a lifetime ago. I'm a peaceable gent nowadays.' The laughter that followed this remark attracted the attention of the waiter. Alfie reckoned folks didn't do much laughing round here.

They returned in splendour in first class and were back home just after midday. Betty greeted him as if he'd been gone a month and not a few hours. Sarah were equally enthusiastic with Robert.

His friend told the whole and the news were received with delight. 'Where's Ma? Why ain't she here to celebrate with us?'

There was an uncomfortable silence. Sarah told him what had happened and he were so shocked that for once in his life he were rendered silent.

'I'm sorry, Alfie, but for her to side with that man after what he did to John is unforgivable.'

'We can't send her away; she's our flesh and blood. Don't mean I like it, but she ain't going anywhere. As long as she keeps to taking care of the children and leaves us be, that'll do me.'

His sister didn't look convinced but then Robert drew her to one side and spoke quietly to her. Whatever he said did the trick.

'Very well, but I shan't be sorry if she decides to move out after the festive period.'

Ada had found a bottle of sweet sherry from somewhere and poured them all a tot. He stood and raised his glass. He were a lucky man to be surrounded by those he loved and to be living in such luxury. They'd a lot to celebrate – Sarah and Robert would be married next week, and he and

Betty would have a babe in the summer. Hatch were gone for good, business were looking up for all of them. He raised his glass, his eyes wet.

'To the Nightingale family, the Coopers and the Billingses. Long may we prosper and enjoy our good fortune. Merry Christmas to you all.'

ABOUT THE AUTHOR

Fenella J. Miller is the bestselling writer of over eighteen historical sagas. She also has a passion for Regency romantic adventures and has published over fifty to great acclaim. Her father was a Yorkshireman and her mother the daughter of a Rajah. She lives in a small village in Essex with her British Shorthair cat.

Sign up to Fenella J. Miller's mailing list for news, competitions and updates on future books.

Visit Fenella's website: www.fenellajmiller.co.uk

Follow Fenella on social media here:

facebook.com/fenella.miller

x.com/fenellawriter

ALSO BY FENELLA J. MILLER

Goodwill House Series

The War Girls of Goodwill House

New Recruits at Goodwill House

Duty Calls at Goodwill House

The Land Girls of Goodwill House

A Wartime Reunion at Goodwill House

Wedding Bells at Goodwill House

A Christmas Baby at Goodwill House

The Army Girls Series

Army Girls Reporting For Duty

Army Girls: Heartbreak and Hope

Army Girls: Behind the Guns

The Pilot's Girl Series

The Pilot's Girl

A Wedding for the Pilot's Girl

A Dilemma for the Pilot's Girl

A Second Chance for the Pilot's Girl

The Nightingale Family Series

A Pocketful of Pennies

A Capful of Courage

A Basket Full of Babies

A Home Full of Hope

Standalone

The Land Girl's Secret

Milton Keynes UK
Ingram Content Group UK Ltd.
UKHW040939080724
445225UK00002B/3

9 781835 187111